"I didn't mean to jump on you earlier,"

Cade said, his gaze drifting to the vee of her robe. "It's just that the boys and I have managed fine for the past three years without any interference."

When she didn't respond, he said, "Aren't you going to say anything?"

She started to move past him. "Good night, Cade."

He clasped her arm. "Say what you're thinking."

"You'll only get angry again, Cade. I think I'll keep my opinion to myself, thank you."

"Don't go all cold and icy on me, Miranda. You're not like that."

She looked at his hand on her arm, then asked softly, "What do you want from me?"

"Damned if I know...."

MARRY ME,
Cowboy

COWBOY AT THE WEDDING
Karen Rose Smith

WRANGLER
DADS

Silhouette Books

Published by Silhouette Books
America's Publisher of Contemporary Romance

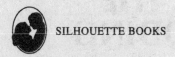

SILHOUETTE BOOKS

RECYCLED PAPER

ISBN 0-373-65314-X

COWBOY AT THE WEDDING

This edition published by arrangement with Harlequin Books S.A.

® and TM are trademarks of Harlequin Books S.A., used under license.
Trademarks indicated with ® are registered in the United States Patent
and Trademark Office, the Canadian Trade Marks Office and in other
countries.

Visit Silhouette at www.eHarlequin.com

Printed in U.S.A.

KAREN ROSE SMITH

Award-winning and bestselling author Karen Rose Smith began reading romances as a teenager. Her favorites included horses. Farms and ranches still beckon to her now that she's an adult. She insists the peace she can find in these settings can't be matched anywhere. She will never pass up the chance to pet and talk to a horse or walk into a barn and smell the wonderful scents of hay, horses and leather! She called up memories from childhood experiences on a relative's farm to write *Cowboy at the Wedding.*

Karen Rose likes to hear from her readers. You can write her at P.O. Box 1545, Hanover, PA 17331 or through her Web site at www.karenrosesmith.com.

To the "Best Men" in my life—my husband, Steve, and my son, Kenny. I love you.

Prologue

Cade Gallagher watched in frustration as the housekeeper's green sedan roared away in a cloud of Montana dust. The door to his house stood ajar. He suspected why. The late-August sun beat on his neck as he climbed the wooden steps to the front porch and hurried inside.

Three pairs of innocent brown eyes stared up at Cade. The wide-eyed culprits were eight, seven and four. Freckles danced across their noses, and if his sons weren't so damned cute...

"I want an explanation *now*," Cade said sternly.

"You're not gonna explode, Dad, are you? Charlie says one of these days it's all gonna come firin' out like Mount Saint Helens." Gregory, his oldest, asked the question seriously.

Cade took him seriously, although it was hard to do when the gap-toothed expression on his son's face led Cade to believe all three boys would love to see the explosion.

Raking his hand through his hair, he calmed himself and took a deep breath. It was the way he'd managed frustration and anger for the past three years. More than anything, he wanted to give his sons a stable childhood. But that was practically impossible with their mother abandoning them and their pranks chasing away every housekeeper he'd hired during the last six months.

Swiping off his black Stetson, he set it on the table without taking his eyes from the three delinquents before him. "I want to know what you did to Mrs. Hunter. She wasn't even here two weeks!"

"Aw, Dad, we didn't do nothin'," Gregory offered.

"You didn't do *anything*," Cade corrected automatically.

"That's what Gregory said," Tim, his middle son, agreed with a nod of his head.

Cade looked around at the state of the kitchen— a measuring cup once full of flour tilted over on the counter, and three pairs of white footprints tracked across the floor. Apparently water had sprayed in all directions; puddles stood everywhere. Aluminum trays of burned cookies lay jumbled diagonally on the table. All of this chaos had occurred in the space of a morning—a morning during which he'd tried to get much-needed work done on the bunkhouse.

Cade knew his best strategy in a situation like this was to aim for the weakest link. Dragging an oak kitchen chair with his foot, he corralled his youngest son and sat him on his lap. "Sean, can you tell me why there's flour all over our kitchen?"

Sean hadn't yet learned the stall tactics of his brothers. "Mrs. Hunter spilled it."

Cade had learned long ago that the secret to getting straight answers from his sons was asking the right questions. "But *why* did she spill it?" He gave Sean one of those fatherly stares that said his four-year-old was staying exactly where he was until he talked.

Sean looked at his brothers, then back at his dad. "Um…'cause…maybe 'cause Tim told her we put sand in the flour and mixed it up real good and was it okay for us to eat sand in our cookies?"

"She spilled **the** flour because you told her it had sand in it. Did the first batch burn because of the sand?" Cade knew the importance of striving for clarity.

"They burned because Gregory set the timer for too long," Timothy reluctantly said when neither Sean nor Gregory answered.

Cade turned his stare on his oldest son—the ringleader. "On purpose?"

Caught, Gregory shifted on his feet. "I was help-ing, is all."

"Helping get rid of Mrs. Hunter?" Cade asked with gentle but demanding authority.

"Aw, Dad…"

This time Cade pinned his middle son with a stare. "And the water?"

Timothy gazed down at his sneakers. "We, uh, loosened the washer. And when she turned it on…"

Thinking up punishment was becoming an exer-cise in creativity. "Boys…"

Sean squirmed off Cade's lap and stood between his older brothers. "We know. We hafta go to our rooms till we can think of all the reasons why we're sorry."

He didn't know whether to laugh or send them to military school. "That will do for starters. I'm sup-posed to leave for a wedding in Washington, D.C., tomorrow. With Mrs. Hunter gone, I might have to cancel the trip."

All three looked genuinely contrite. Gregory said, "We're sorry, Dad. But Charlie can stay with us. Then you can still be Uncle Jeff's best man."

Any other time, Cade would cancel the trip. But he hadn't seen Jeff, Gavin and Nathan in a long while. It had been years since they'd all been to-gether in one place at the same time. Fraternity brothers. Friends. Although time and distance separated them, when they connected again, it was like old times. Almost.

Now, responsibility weighed heavily on Cade's shoulders. He loved his three boys. He loved his Montana ranch that had been an adventure during the summers when he was a boy and his uncle had taught him roping, riding, and a sense of achievement.

He wanted to give that same sense of achievement to his sons. Although Charlie—who'd worked on the ranch ever since Cade could remember—was getting older, he could handle the boys for three days, and that was probably what his offspring had intended all along.

"All right. I'll let Charlie take over while I'm gone. But I'm going to call every night, and I'd better hear that all of you have done your chores and are helping rather than hindering."

"What's 'hindering,' Dad?" Sean innocently asked.

Tim nudged him. "It means not gettin' in the way."

Cade just shook his head. When he came home, he'd have to start the search for another housekeeper all over again. What woman in her right mind would want to take on this crew?

Chapter One

"The maid of honor's finally here," Jeff Stanhope announced to Cade, Nathan and Gavin as he hurried into the small room behind the church's altar. "I knew Miranda would make it on time."

Cade pulled at the stiff collar around his neck. "Nothing like cutting it down to the wire. What did you say she does?"

"She's a defense attorney. She used to work with Katie at the legal-aid office here in D.C. But then a New York firm offered her a partnership. It's hard for her to get away."

"If she's Katie's maid of honor, you'd think she'd take a couple of days off."

Jeff adjusted his boutonniere so it was perfectly straight. "Like you would have taken a couple of days off while you worked as a stockbroker?" His friend's sly smile when he raised his head told Cade that Jeff had a long memory.

Cade's collar pulled even tighter. Five years ago he'd laid aside suits, ties, and Italian-leather shoes and never looked back. Unlike his ex-wife. "I just meant…"

Gavin slapped Cade on the shoulder and winked at Jeff. "You expect too much from women. You always have."

Cade bristled. Then, seeing the knowing smiles on his three old friends' faces, he grimaced. "That might have been true in the past. Now, I don't expect anything so I'm not disappointed." He saw the looks Gavin, Nathan and Jeff exchanged. They knew the toll his divorce had taken on him and also on his perspective. They knew he didn't associate "happy" and "marriage" together anymore.

But this day wasn't about him. It was about Jeff and Katie and their hopes for the future. Maybe Jeff had found what Cade never could—a woman to share the same dreams. "So what do I have to do with…Miranda?" he asked.

Jeff grinned. "Just what we practiced last night with the other bridesmaids. When Miranda reaches the altar, she'll stand on the left with them. We'll already be on the right. At the recessional you escort her out. Just relax, Cade. Women are good at these things."

* * *

As best man, Cade stood at the altar beside Jeff and waited. The church's air-conditioning system made the tuxedo bearable, but Cade missed his jeans and boots almost as much as he missed his sons.

The organist began the wedding march and Cade suddenly realized everything about this wedding was tastefully elegant rather than overdone. Jeff had said that Katie had planned it all, from the white gladiolus on the altar to the candles stationed at the pews.

Music filled the small church on a rising crescendo. The first bridesmaid started down the white runner. Instead of swishing material fashioned in a long skirt, she wore a blue-green suit with a neck shaped like a heart. Katie's touch again, probably. These were all professional women.

The second bridesmaid walked down the aisle and took her place beside the first.

The maid of honor appeared.

As she moved forward, Cade stared. It was the same suit, the same neckline, the same straight skirt, the same color, but on her the material seemed to shimmer. Maybe because of her auburn hair smoothed back from her face, maybe because of her smile that told the world she was proud to be a friend of this couple, maybe because of the flicker of the candles that gave her fair skin a porcelain glow. When she reached the altar, Cade felt as if a bucking bronco had dumped him in the dust and the fall had knocked the air from his lungs.

Her gaze met his and held.

So *this* was Miranda.

She reached the altar, then stepped to the left, leaving the aisle behind free for the bride's special moment.

Katie was a beautiful bride in white lace, but after she stood beside her husband-to-be at the altar, Cade glanced again at Miranda. Her hair was woven into an intricate twist. Soft tendrils floated along her face. The noon light streaming through the sanctuary windows caught the red fire in her hair. With the self-discipline Cade had honed since he was a teenager completing chores on his uncle's ranch, he ignored the stabs of basic desire and concentrated on the minister and the happiness of the couple beside him.

An hour after the ceremony, receiving line, and photographs, Miranda sat at the long banquet table and sipped at her champagne, feeling as if she'd dashed through the past week at supersonic speed. Ever since she'd moved to New York...

She sighed. Success. That's what her father had always encouraged. He'd wanted it for her, and she'd thought she'd wanted it, too. After all, her two brothers were successful. Didn't she have to keep up? Didn't she have to prove she was as good as they were? To whom? To herself? To her father? And why was all this coming up now?

Maybe it was Katie and Jeff's wedding. Maybe it

was the excitement in her stomach whenever she looked at the best man. He seemed to stir up a restlessness she hadn't known existed. It was ridiculous. She was dating someone—someone prestigious, someone her father approved of. David was the vice president of an advertising agency. He understood her drive to succeed and make a reputation for herself. He'd even brought her her latest client, and it was a high-profile case.

She snuck a peek at the best man again. Actually, he wasn't handsome. But he emanated a rugged masculinity she found compelling. By the way Cade Gallagher had kept pulling his collar away from his neck through the photograph session, the toast and dinner, she guessed he disliked the formality of a tuxedo. At six-two, in stark black-and-white, his dark brown hair shaggier than that of the two groomsmen who were obviously his friends as well as the groom's, he seemed to dominate the room where he stood, whether it was the chapel Katie and Jeff had chosen for their ceremony or the reception hall of the hotel.

She remembered the instant her gaze had met his as she reached the altar. She remembered the moment they'd met in the back of the church before the receiving line formed.

She'd extended her hand and introduced herself. ''I'm Miranda Sinclair.''

His hand had enfolded hers; it had been strong

and engulfing, his dark brown eyes deep and intense. "I know. I'm Cade Gallagher."

She'd smiled. "I know." Katie had given her a very brief biography of Jeff's best man, simply saying he lived on a ranch in Montana although he'd once worked in New York City.

Then Cade's fingers had tightened slightly as he studied Miranda's face. Her knees seemed wobbly and she'd told herself the weakness came strictly from hunger. She'd rushed to make her flight and hadn't eaten all day.

Abruptly, their brief contact had been interrupted by the duties of the bridal party, although when Cade had released her hand, the sensation of his touch had lingered.

Now, at the banquet table, separated from Cade Gallagher by Katie and Jeff, Miranda wanted to know more about him.

Suddenly Cade pushed back his chair and stood, murmured something to Jeff, and disappeared through the double doors that led to a glassed-in porch. Miranda could see his profile as he stood next to a post and stared over the gardens.

Katie leaned over to Miranda. "Jeff and I are going to mingle before we cut the cake. What time do you have to leave?"

Miranda checked the petite gold watch on her wrist. "Around three."

Katie stood. "Just don't you leave without saying goodbye."

Miranda squeezed her friend's hand. "I won't."

As everyone at the table stood and scattered, Miranda found herself headed for the doors to the porch.

She let them close silently behind her and asked Cade, "Do you mind some company?"

He gave her a sort of half smile and a look of appreciative male interest that made her heart beat faster.

Miranda walked over to the side of the porch where he stood. Fuchsia and white impatiens circled a birdbath in the center of the garden. "Katie said you live on a ranch in Montana."

He nodded.

She stole a sideways glance at him. "Do you like having all that space around you?"

"That's why I moved there."

A man of few words. Most of the men she knew talked politics, law and business every chance they got. An inner urge told her to push a little more, to nudge a little harder. If she didn't, this man would probably be able to carry on the conversation without saying much at all. She wanted to know more than the little bit Katie had told her.

Facing him, knowing surprise was usually the best ammunition when a client or witness was reluctant to open up, she said, "I was wondering if you're as silent as you are solemn."

His brows arched.

She could tell he used silence to speak for him or not speak for him. So much for tactics that *usually* worked. Trying again, she prodded, "Most guests at a wedding smile quite a bit."

"Not many marriages make it these days." His posture was relaxed, but she sensed a challenge in his reply. He dared her to contradict him.

Should she or shouldn't she ask the obvious question? She decided she should. "Are you married?"

That brought a tilt of his head and a penetrating look. "Divorced. What about you?"

"Never married."

He rested his hand on the support post by her shoulder. "Jeff said you're a very busy lawyer."

So when he talked, he made a point. She heard censure in his tone. Instead of annoying her, his words made that restless feeling inside her increase to a longing for something else. It made her wonder why she attended social functions with David and mingled more than she spent time with him. And why he did the same. "My career is my life."

Cade's brown eyes deepened. "Is that the way you want it?"

Something about his stance, the gentleness in his voice, told her he knew about work being one's life. "I'm not sure anymore." Turning the tables, she asked, "What keeps you busy besides your ranch?"

"Do you think it's not enough?"

He would make a good lawyer—he knew how to take the offensive and keep it. "No. I'd imagine it's a twenty-four-hour-a-day job. But if you realize there's more to life than work..." She trailed off to give him an easy opening.

"What if I said, 'Wine, women and song'?" His expression was deliberately neutral.

"It doesn't fit." She smiled. "You're too solemn."

He chuckled. "You're good."

With a small shrug, she responded, "It's part of my job to read people."

He nodded as if he understood. After a few moments of silence, he said, "My three boys make me laugh more often than wine, women and song ever could. They also give me more headaches."

He was a divorced father, but he had custody of his children. Another surprise. "How old are they?"

"Eight, seven and four, and lately as ornery as they come. They've run off the last four housekeepers I've hired."

She laughed. "My goodness. What kind of women do you hire?"

He looked out over her shoulder into the garden. "Possibly the same kind as their mother. Women who leave when the going gets tough."

She heard the bitterness. "How long has it been since your wife left?"

He went silent, then finally answered, "Three years."

She realized Cade Gallagher wasn't the type of man to answer personal questions easily. But they were two strangers who would go their separate ways. He was answering her questions because he knew he'd probably never see her again, and perhaps because he was too polite to tell her to mind her own business. Or maybe because he needed to talk to someone. She would guess he solved his own problems and didn't ask for help until there were no other solutions. "Three boys take a lot of care."

He nodded. "We had a woman they latched on to like a grandmother. But she was called back to Seattle to help her mother. Since then... Well, let's just say I try to keep the chaos from getting out of hand." He met her gaze then. "You don't happen to know a good housekeeper, do you?" he asked with a wry smile that said he was looking wherever he could.

She could get lost in those eyes. So deep. So penetrating. She shook her head. "There are nanny services in New York."

He dropped his hand from the post and slid it into his trouser pocket. "I know, but I'd rather hire someone who comes recommended. Though that hasn't been an advantage up to now," he admitted in a dry tone. "And Montana isn't a state where many people want to settle. Especially women."

She saw the deep pain in his eyes that went along with the phrase he'd tacked on. "Right now, Montana's wide spaces and big sky sound like a bit of heaven."

"You need an escape?" he asked with a perception that didn't surprise her.

"I wish I had time for an escape."

"Sometimes you have to take the time." He leaned a little closer. "If you don't, you can lose yourself."

Without knowing how or why, they'd gone from simply friendly to a deeper level that had to do with life, changes, and decisions that mattered. "Did you lose yourself?" she asked.

Cocking his head, he admitted, "I was on my way. My dream kept me going, but day-to-day life on Wall Street was dragging me down."

She breathed in his cologne, but something else much more masculine and vital, too. "What was the dream?"

When he smiled he looked younger. "To be a cowboy."

His honest answer awakened needs inside her to find her own dream and let it bring her joy.

"You aren't laughing," he said, his voice husky.

"I don't laugh at dreams," she said softly, knowing how precious dreams were and how carefully they should be cherished.

His gaze locked with hers and suddenly dreams

became much more important than reality. She had never felt such an elemental pull toward a man as she did toward Cade Gallagher. In her career she'd met, socialized, and worked with scores of men, but none had intrigued her like this one. And none had created the urge to move closer, talk more, feel his arms around her.

"Your eyes are the same color as your suit," he commented, his voice low and incredibly exciting.

It took her a moment to manage, "Sometimes they're bluer than others."

He studied her more thoroughly. "The color reminds me of a mountain lake at dawn."

She trembled from the power in his gaze and the compliment. She guessed he didn't give them often to women.

They stared into each other's eyes. For that moment they understood each other perfectly, and they wanted the same thing—to explore the pull, to capture the moment, to forget about time, responsibilities and anything else but now. Usually, she didn't give in to impulses; didn't meet a man and want...

When Cade bent his head, she knew exactly what she wanted.

They came together in mutual surprise. When his lips parted, she responded by inviting him in. The tip of his tongue brushed hers, and she lost all sense of time and place. Then he did something no man had ever done. Instead of closing her in a tight embrace, instead of groping for further intimacy, she felt his hand on her face, stroking her, reassuring her, yet exciting her. It was a lovely hello, yet it held the touch of goodbye, too. This was one moment snatched from everyday life, and they knew they would probably never see each other again. Was that why the kiss held so much passion, curiosity and…freedom?

When Cade pulled away, they stared at each other and waited.

Finally Cade said, "Strange things happen at weddings."

Miranda smiled. "Or nice things."

Offhandedly, as if he wasn't sure what should happen next, he suggested, "If you're ever in Montana, look me up. Maybe I can show you a little bit of heaven."

His kiss had. It had been a surprise, a joy and a respite in a life that sometimes seemed as steep as a cliff. Although a vacation in Montana qualified as another dream, she didn't hesitate to say, "I will."

One of the double doors opened. Gavin strode in like a forceful wind. "C'mon, you two. It's time for the wedding party to dance." He exited as fast as he'd entered.

Cade shook his head. "Just like a doctor. Gives an order and expects everyone to follow it."

Miranda laughed. "Have you known him long?"

"Same as Jeff and Nathan. Since college."

The sound of voices from the reception hall vibrated through the glass. When Miranda's eyes collided with Cade's, she realized that their conversation and whatever else had ignited between them was coming to an end.

Through the steady murmur outside the doors, someone called their names.

"We can't disappoint Katie and Jeff." Cade offered her his arm. "Would you like to dance?"

Miranda nodded. She was used to delivering opening statements and summations, arguing a point of law, cross-examining a witness even when information surfaced that surprised her. She always kept her composure. So why couldn't she find an intelligent word to say now? At a loss, she simply took Cade's arm.

The bridal party waited for Cade and Miranda to reach the dance floor. With no awkwardness whatsoever, Cade took her in his arms. He was as strong and muscled as she'd suspected, although his hold was loose. She could smell his after-shave and feel his heat through the tuxedo jacket. As the couples began to dance, he drew her closer. It was only a dance, she told herself. She and David had never made any promises, had never made love.

Why? She couldn't imagine being with this man and not wanting to—

She cut off the thought and was scandalized by it. What was happening to her?

He used hand pressure to guide her, and she had no problem following. Katie and Jeff brushed past them. Miranda tilted her chin up. "They're in their own world."

Close to her ear, Cade murmured, "I hope it lasts for them."

His breath was warm, caressing. The material of his jacket was stiff under her fingers. But she could feel the man underneath. Her heart raced. Being held close to him was exciting, more exciting than she could ever imagine. She leaned back and their gazes caught and held. For a moment Miranda couldn't breathe.

"Are you staying at the hotel tonight?" he asked.

She saw the golden desire in his brown eyes and she felt an answering response. This wasn't like her. She didn't get attracted to men this way. She didn't meet them one minute, kiss them the next, and think about—

Someone tapped her on the shoulder, breaking her train of thought, breaking the mood, breaking the compelling attraction to Cade. Turning slightly, she saw a bellboy.

"Your limousine has arrived, Miss Sinclair. Shall I tell the driver you're ready?"

But she wasn't ready. She—

Cade released her and took a step away. "You *are* a busy lady."

Where she could read Cade Gallagher before, now

she couldn't. His brown eyes held his thoughts in secret, and his expression showed neither surprise nor disappointment.

She found herself making an excuse—something she seldom did. "I have to get back tonight. I'm due in court first thing Monday morning, and I need tomorrow to prepare."

Cade remained silent.

Miranda smiled, hoping to coax a smile from him. "It was a pleasure meeting you, talking to you, and…" She trailed off. How did a woman thank a man for a magnificent kiss? "I have to tell Katie and Jeff goodbye."

Still, he just stared. No smile. No acknowledgment that he'd enjoyed the time with her as much as she'd enjoyed the time with him.

The bellboy stood waiting. She said to him, "Tell the driver I'll be out in five minutes."

Finally, Cade spoke. "Good luck."

"With my court case?" she asked.

"No. With your busy life." And he walked away.

Adding frozen green beans to the boiling water, Cade knew Gregory and Tim would eat them, Sean wouldn't. So he took a package of frozen peas from the freezer and poured them into another pot. It would be a hell of a lot easier if they all ate with the hands in the bunkhouse kitchen. But that wasn't the place for his boys to grow up learning manners or realizing that vegetables should be an important part of their diet. Charlie was a whiz at cooking food that made Al and Buck happy. But little boys were a different matter, although his sons didn't agree. They'd eat corn bread and beans every night if he'd let them.

Cade had gotten Tim and Gregory settled in their room with their homework. Sean was coloring. So he had about a half hour to get dinner on the table. If he was lucky. Thank goodness school had started. At least he didn't have to worry about Tim and Gregory during the day. But soon, he had to find a solution to him and Charlie juggling taking care of Sean.

The phone rang, and Cade picked up the receiver while he lifted the lid on the peas. "Hello."

"Mr. Gallagher? It's Miranda Sinclair."

Cade dropped the lid onto the stove where it clanked against the spoon rest.

She rushed on. "Katie gave me your number. She said you wouldn't mind."

Mind? He'd thought about Miranda Sinclair a lot in the past month since the wedding. He'd dreamed about her, too. Vivid, hot dreams where they were doing more than dancing. But in the morning he'd dismissed the dreams, and during the day he'd chased the thoughts away with pressing concerns. She wasn't his type of woman. He wasn't her type of man. If she needed or wanted a man at all, Cade was sure he'd be CEO of a Fortune 500 company.

"How can I help you, Miranda?"

"I decided to take that vacation. I'm...uh...in Billings. I wondered if your invitation to visit is still open?"

Cade had dreamed about Miranda Sinclair, but he'd never imagined she would actually land in his backyard. There was something in her voice—a vulnerability he hadn't heard while they'd talked at the reception. "Is something wrong, Miranda?"

The silence told him before she spoke. "I needed to get out of New York. I needed to...get away for a while."

The desperation he heard didn't seem in character. "Was your life in danger?" He'd lived in New York a lifetime ago. But he could still remember the schemes, the risks, the fortunes involved.

This time her silence worried him even more than the desperation. "Miranda?"

"Not physically." She sighed. "I'm being overly dramatic. You probably think I'm a very strange woman, calling you out of the blue like this."

"What happened?" Something had shaken her.

"Let's just say I've been reevaluating my life. My very busy life. I needed a vacation and I thought of...Montana. Actually, I thought while I got a break from New York maybe I could help you out. Katie said you still hadn't found a nanny."

He pictured her as he'd seen her at the wedding—upswept hair, pearls at her ears, perfectly manicured and polished nails. "I need someone permanent."

"Oh, I understand. But I thought maybe I could fill in instead of being a bother while I'm around."

She'd bother his libido more than anything else. "Miranda, staying on a ranch with three hellions scurrying around will not be a vacation."

"I practically raised my two younger brothers. Your three can't be any more mischievous than they were."

As if on cue, Sean ran into the kitchen and latched on to his father's legs. Gregory came running after him. "He's got my pencil!"

Sean peeked at his brother from behind Cade. "I do not. Tim has it." The youngest pointed at Tim who stood in the doorway. "He broke my crayon."

"I did not. You put it in front of my foot. I can't help it if I stepped on it."

"Cade. Are you there?" Miranda asked.

He was there, all right.

Sean yelled at Tim, Gregory defended his brother, and as happened most days, all hell broke loose.

And as usual, when Cade had had enough, he yelled into the fray, "Gentlemen!"

The three boys stopped squabbling and stared up at him.

"I'm on the phone. Either stand there quietly until I finish or go back to your room."

Gregory and Tim vanished and clomped up the stairs. Sean leaned against Cade's left leg.

He certainly could use some help. What harm could it do to let Miranda Sinclair help him out while she escaped from her life for a little while. "Where are you?"

She named a hotel in Billings.

"I'll come and get you tomorrow around three. But, Miranda, after a day here, you might decide a hotel is a much more pleasant place to be."

She laughed. "Have a little faith, Cade."

Oh, he had faith, all right—faith that Miranda Sinclair wouldn't find enough blue sky to make up for the shenanigans of his boys, the long days, and the demands of ranch life. She might last a few days. He certainly wouldn't bet on more.

Chapter Two

In the hours since Cade had spoken to Miranda on the telephone, he'd told himself she couldn't possibly be as pretty as he remembered. As he entered the hotel and glanced toward the elevators, he looked for the elegant woman he'd met at the wedding.

Suddenly a woman stood before him. He took a second look.

She asked, "Cade?"

All right. So what had he expected? A silk suit and spike heels? His gaze drifted from the braid dangling over Miranda Sinclair's shoulder, down the blue-and-gray striped sweater with the sleeves pushed up her forearms, to the jeans that showed off her figure much better than the suit she'd worn at the wedding. Running shoes completed her outfit.

"Miranda?"

She smiled and nodded. "But for vacation purposes how about if you call me Randi?"

He lifted his head and made eye contact. "Randi?"

"Short for Miranda. My brothers liked to think of me as one of the guys. Hopefully your boys will, too."

One of the guys. She had to be kidding. "Don't tell me you were a tomboy."

"Not exactly. But I could climb a tree with the best of them."

Cade needed to do some mental readjustment, though not a lot. Miranda's—Randi's hair still looked silky and touchable. She was still every inch a woman. And if he knew what was good for him, he'd ignore that fact while she was his guest. He picked up her suitcase.

She looked up at him, her aquamarine eyes clear and dazzling. "You didn't bring the boys with you?"

"They're supposed to be cleaning their room so they can impress you."

"Your idea or theirs?"

He grimaced. "Mine, of course. Charlie's watching them, but I thought that would keep them out of his hair."

She shifted her travel bag to her other hand. "Who's Charlie?"

"He used to be my uncle's right hand, but now he's a general troubleshooter and cook for the hands."

She looked puzzled. "Your uncle lives with you?"

Cade started walking toward the exit. "No. He died five years ago and left me the ranch." He stopped suddenly. "Is this your only luggage?"

"Yes. I...left in a hurry."

To evade Cade's probing stare, she crossed to the revolving glass door.

Randi stared out the window of Cade's four-wheel drive vehicle. They passed prairie grasslands, cattle ranches, rock formations carved by the elements. She'd never been farther west than Chicago. The colors here welcomed her into their folds—the bright blue sky, the autumn reds, warm russets and golds of the last of the foliage on larch, aspen and birch. She'd never seen such vast sweeps of land that seemed to know no boundaries. Cade had told her the trip to the ranch would take about an hour and a half. Then he'd fallen silent.

Why had she told Cade Gallagher to call her Randi? Because she wanted to separate herself from the defense attorney who'd left New York? Because she couldn't trust "Miranda's" judgment and she felt more comfortable as "Randi," with none of her father's expectations and all of her brothers' affection and camaraderie?

That was as good an explanation as any.

She was trying to forget—about her inability to evaluate character accurately, David's betrayal, the guilt of the client she'd thought was innocent...and finally, her father's anger. All of it had closed in on her until the idea of leaving her life in New York behind had seemed the only solution.

For someone who had never acted capriciously, her decision to call Katie for the location of Cade's ranch and the sudden flight to Billings had been a strange impulse. But ever since the wedding she'd wondered how to fit a trip to Montana into her schedule. And when her world had come crashing down, she'd pictured Cade's steady brown eyes, remembered the feel of his hand on her face, and relived their kiss. If he didn't want her here, she could always leave. But for now, maybe they could both do each other a favor. Randi suspected Cade had thought "Miranda" wouldn't last on his ranch for a day. Well, he was wrong, no matter which persona she used. Helping Cade take care of his sons would take plenty of physical energy. Hopefully, at night she would be able to forget New York, underhanded dealings, and men who lied even as they were trying to romance. Or especially when they were trying to romance. She'd been a fool. She'd almost put her career in jeopardy, not to mention her heart.

When she'd come home from her meeting with the district attorney last week—shaken, betrayed, and sad—she'd known it was time to reevaluate her life before she lost herself in work and cynicism forever. What better place to do it than in the vast open land of Montana.

"Tell me about the ranch," she suggested, simply to make conversation as she watched Cade's hands on the steering wheel. His fingers were long but sturdy. His palms were broad. When he'd shaken her hand after the wedding, when he'd touched her face, she'd felt calluses. Her gaze followed his arm to his shoulders and profile. His complexion carried a tan that probably lasted all winter.

"It's mostly grazing land. The western boundary stretches into the mountains. The house itself is a one-and-a-half-story with three bedrooms, two up and one down. Yours will be downstairs. There's only a half bath on the first floor. You'll have to go upstairs to bathe or shower."

Over and over, she'd wondered about his question while they were dancing. *Are you staying at the hotel tonight?* he'd asked. What would have happened if she'd stayed? Would they have shared conversation over a cup of coffee…dinner…more? No. She wasn't that type of woman. In spite of the unexpected kiss, she didn't think he was that type of man. He also wasn't the type of man to dish out a polished line with practiced sincerity as David had.

"Katie and Jeff told me about your house."

He glanced at her sideways. "Oh, they did? What else did they tell you?"

She didn't know if she heard amusement or annoyance. "When I asked Jeff about you, he said you're a moral man who works hard and wants the best for your sons. That's a high compliment."

Cade glanced at her briefly, then stared at the road before them.

A short time later he turned right off the road and drove down a lane. In a few minutes, he pulled up in front of a log house, the front part of which was surrounded by a wraparound porch. A sugar maple stood in the front yard with a tire hanging from one of its boughs.

"This is charming! I love the porch."

"My uncle built it. He made those chairs, too."

Ladder-back chairs sat around a pine table. There was such pride in Cade's voice, not only about his uncle but whenever he spoke of the ranch. Randi was eager to explore and opened her door. Across from the house, a barn, a barrackslike structure, and various outbuildings stood against the expansive blue sky. No one milled about.

As if Cade had read her mind, he said, "The hands are repairing fence. Saturday night, they go into town." Then he climbed out and came around to her door. "Meeting Charlie and my sons will be enough for one evening. I'll show you around the ranch tomorrow.''

She couldn't tell if he was trying to scare her or prepare her.

Carrying her suitcase in one hand, as if it held nothing heavier than cotton balls, Cade walked beside her to the house. He let her precede him up the porch steps. ''The door should be open,'' he said.

She was used to dead bolts and steel doors. This wooden one was slightly ajar. She took the knob and began to push the door.

Randi didn't know what happened first. She heard squeals as she felt something cold and wet splash over her head, down her face and all over her clothes. Just as suddenly she saw a bucket miss her shoulder by an inch and bounce to the floor. The shock of cold water made her gasp for breath and water went up her nose. She coughed and sputtered.

Cade swore and feet scurried away amid giggles before she'd realized what had happened.

''Are you all right?'' Concern and apology filled his voice.

She opened her eyes, not realizing until that moment that she'd closed them. Her eyelashes dripped water as did her hair. Wiping her hands over her nose, she said, ''I thought you didn't have a shower downstairs.''

Cade wasn't amused by her attempt at humor.

"Did that bucket hit you?" His forehead creased with worry as he examined her closely.

"No, it didn't. It missed my shoulder—"

Cade's bellow shook the house. "Gregory, Timothy and Sean Gallagher! Get in here!"

The three boys appeared one at a time in the doorway and huddled close together.

Cade pointed to the door. "The three of you. Out there on the porch on the chairs. And don't move until I get there. Do you understand?"

Cade's exasperated tone would have intimidated her, but the boys looked more embarrassed than afraid.

"Dad," Gregory started.

"Not a word," Cade warned.

The three traded looks and marched toward the door. At the threshold the youngest asked his brothers, "Did he 'splode?"

The oldest nudged the youngest and said, "Shh."

Randi heard chair legs scrape on the wooden porch, but nothing else.

"One of these days they're going to learn there are consequences to their pranks. One of these days—"

"Cade, do you have a towel?"

She didn't think his dark scowl was strictly for her, but he ordered her the same way he'd ordered the boys. "Don't move."

Apparently he was used to giving orders. "Just

where do you think I'm going to go?'' she asked
sweetly.

He swore again, mumbled something about Charlie that wasn't complimentary, and strode out of the
kitchen. A few moments later, he returned with a
bath-size green towel. Instead of handing it to her,
he wrapped it around her shoulders. ''Mir—Randi,
I'm sorry. That was quite a welcome and I'll understand if—''

''I want to sue?''

He looked horror-stricken.

She smiled. ''I'm kidding. Lighten up, Mr. Gallagher. A little water never hurt anyone.''

He stared at her as if she were out of her mind.
Then she realized he was holding the towel together
over her breasts. As he realized it, too, his eyes became mysterious and deep, making her want to explore him—his thoughts, his desires. He wiped a
drop of water from her cheek.

A tremor quivered through her from the touch of
his finger. The pad of his thumb was rough, but so
gentle.

''I can't tell if you're being a good sport or mock-
ing me.''

''Maybe a little of both.'' She wondered if she
sounded as breathless as she felt.

''You're a difficult woman to read, Miss Sinclair.''

''Maybe you're trying too hard.'' A shiver swept

through her from the rivulets of water skittering down her neck.

"You're cold." He tightened the towel around her shoulders.

She was hot and cold and much too aware of a sexy rancher she would be sharing a house with. Her hand covered his as she strove to take the towel from him. But she forgot about the towel as his heat singed her.

Cade released the terry cloth and stepped back. She caught the towel and breathed a sigh of relief.

"Come on upstairs and get a shower," he suggested. "I don't want you to catch pneumonia. Then you *might* sue. While you get warm, I'll deal with the desperadoes on the porch."

She took a quick peek at the living room as she crossed to the stairs. It was homey, with a long couch covered by a patchwork quilt and chairs that looked comfortable and big enough to sleep in. The tables were haphazardly placed for convenience.

Randi's sneakers squeaked on the wooden steps as Cade followed her to the second floor. He said, "I put out clean towels and a new bar of soap for you this morning."

When Randi reached the bathroom, she stepped inside. But before she closed the door, she said to Cade, "Don't be too hard on your sons. They were just having some fun."

Cade just arched his brows, said, "Yell if you need anything," and went downstairs.

A short time later, wrapped in the green towel, Randi opened the bathroom door a crack. She had a problem. Her suitcase was downstairs. The lawyer in her quickly told her to examine her options.

Option one—go downstairs like this. Definitely not. Option two—stay in the bathroom until someone came upstairs. She could be waiting awhile. Option three—sneak into Cade's bedroom and find something to wear. Option four—yell for him as he'd suggested. That seemed the safest.

Opening the door about six inches, she called Cade's name. Then waited. She called again a little louder. Then waited. Venturing to the top of the stairs, she practically yelled. Then waited.

So much for the safest option.

Out in the hall, she decided to find Cade's room. If he got mad, he got mad. She wasn't going downstairs like this. Bad enough her hair was wet, but the towel barely covered her thighs. Opening one of the two closed doors, she found the boys' room. Bunk beds sat against one wall. A single bed stood against another. Socks in variegated colors straggled near the beds as well as a belt, two striped knit shirts, a pair of pajamas and three pairs of slippers. The dresser held assorted treasures—from baseball cards to action figures and comic books.

She smiled. Just like her brothers' room used to look.

Closing that door, she opened the one across the hall, feeling like an intruder. Where the boys' room was cluttered, Cade's room looked stark. A four-poster bed, armoire and desk, all with the patina of antiques, contrasted with the white walls. A computer sat to one side on the desk, a printer on a low table beside it. Blinds rather than curtains covered the windows. A comforter that looked handmade was draped over the mattress, hanging only as far as the frame. Randi crossed to the closet and put her hand on the knob.

The door to Cade's room suddenly opened and he strode in, stopping when he saw her.

Her hand went to her breasts where she'd tucked the end of the towel. "Hi. I didn't mean to trespass, but…" She couldn't think of what to say next, not with him looking at her like a mountain cat about to devour his favorite prey.

He came into the room toward the closet. The closer he got, the more nervous she felt.

"I…uh…need something to wear. My clothes—" she pointed toward the bathroom "—are wet."

"I like what you're wearing." His gaze drifted slowly over her breasts to her bare feet. Then he stepped even closer. "You are one beautiful woman, Randi. Nobody would ever mistake you for a tree-climbing tomboy."

Her throat, her mouth, her lips went dry. It was very hard to swallow, let alone breathe. Cade's hair fell roguishly over his forehead. A swirl of brown curls peeked at her from the open collar of his gray Western-cut shirt. His stomach was as flat as his silver belt buckle, and she bet it was as hard as the oak desk. His jeans hugged his hips and thighs, and his boots added to his sturdy physique. He was all man. And she was standing practically naked in his bedroom.

She should be afraid, and she was. But not of him. She was afraid of herself and the sudden yearnings that overwhelmed her as she gazed at his mouth.

He bent his head, braced one hand on the wall beside her, and she thought perhaps he might…

Cade couldn't remember the last time he'd been so easily aroused by a woman. The slow burn in his gut had begun the moment he'd laid eyes on Miranda before she'd walked down the aisle. There was no explanation for it. Sure, she was a beautiful woman. But he'd seen beautiful women before. Friends had tried to fix him up after Susan left, but he'd shown no interest. He'd felt no interest. They certainly hadn't aroused him.

But this woman was as cool and sophisticated as a princess one minute, as sexy as a barmaid the next. Lordy, what had he gotten himself into? Maybe he should hope his sons and the rigors of ranch life would quickly run her off. He sure as hell didn't want to get involved with her...not with anyone. He'd experienced enough heartache and bitter fights to last a lifetime.

Resisting temptation and a longing he told himself was purely physical, he straightened and opened the closet door. He'd love to see her buttoned into one of his shirts, but that would be as bad as the damned towel. With an impatient jerk, he plucked his navy terry-cloth robe from its hanger and held it out to her. It could cover her twice.

"Put this on and come downstairs. I took your suitcase to your bedroom. I'm sorry I left you up here without clothes." Boy, was he sorry.

She took the robe and held it in front of her. "No problem."

Cade wished that were true.

Charlie stood in Cade's kitchen, his weathered face wrinkled with sincere apology. "Cade, I didn't know what they was doin'. They said they'd behave while I—" Charlie stopped in mid-sentence when Randi walked into the kitchen.

Cade almost smiled. Whether dolled up or wearing a blouse and jeans like she was now, she could stop traffic. And seemed to care less about it. So unlike Susan. So...

"Is there anything I can do to help with supper?"

Cade liked her hair in a ponytail rather than a braid. He'd like to see it loose around her face. "Everything's under control for the moment. Charlie, this is Miranda Sinclair.''

The older man swiped his battered hat from his head. "Hello, Miss Sinclair. Cade, here, told me what happened. I only went to the barn for a few minutes—" He shook his head. "You gotta watch those young'uns every second."

Randi smiled. "I understand. Where are they now?"

"Mucking out stalls," Cade replied with a grim expression.

"Even Sean?"

"Even Sean. Don't let his age fool you. He can conspire with the best of them." Cade could tell Randi was trying to suppress a smile. She might think it was funny now, but give her a week. He'd been dealing with their mischief since Grace left.

The kitchen door swung open and the three boys tumbled inside. "We washed up in the bunkhouse like you said, Dad, and put our shoes on the—" Gregory stopped when he saw Randi.

Tim leaned toward his older brother and said, "She's prettier dry."

Charlie coughed and mumbled, "I've got to get back to the bunkhouse." He couldn't quite hide his grin as he slapped his hat on his head.

Cade rolled his eyes and shook his head, noticing that Randi was biting her lower lip to keep from smiling. Her lips were so perfect, so sweetly curved....

The boys hung their jackets on the wooden pegs at their level behind the door. "Dad, do we hafta 'pologize now?" Sean asked.

Cade cleared his throat, corralling thoughts that were becoming much too frequent. "This would be a good time."

The three boys lined up at the table like choirboys. One after the other they said, "I'm sorry."

Cade wasn't satisfied but it was the best he was going to get at the moment. "Boys, this is Miranda Sinclair. Our guest," Cade said.

"You can call me Randi," she suggested with a smile.

The boys glanced at each other, either puzzled by the name or the smile on her face despite her drenching.

Randi took Gregory's hand and shook it. "It's nice to meet you." Then she did the same with Tim and Sean.

"Okay, boys, it's time for dinner."

Each scrambled to a seat. Tim whispered something to Gregory and the older boy nodded and mumbled, "Yeah. We still are."

Cade smelled trouble. Once in a while he could outthink the trio, but sometimes he just had to wait until disaster happened and take care of them then. He kept his eyes on them throughout dinner, looking for anything suspicious. But he had no cause to correct them. They were quiet and only spoke when spoken to. But with a stranger at the table, that was no surprise.

Randi tried to engage the boys in conversation, but they gave monosyllabic answers except for Sean. To make up for their silence, Cade told Randi more about the ranch, explaining how he and the hands brought the cows to different pastures for winter about two weeks after roundup.

Tim asked, "Is there dessert?"

"Do you think you gentlemen deserve any?" Cade prompted.

Gregory said solemnly, "No, Dad. We don't. But maybe our guest would like a piece of that candy Laura and Ned gave you for your birthday."

"And maybe each of you could have a piece, too?" Cade asked.

"Whatever you say, Dad." Tim looked like an apologetic angel.

The promise of one of those imported chocolates from their closest neighbors could make his sons behave for at least an hour. "All right. I'll get them."

Gregory hopped up. "I'll get 'em, Dad. You keep talking."

Maybe mucking out the stalls had finally brought his point home.

Gregory went to the living room and came back with the box of chocolates. With an engaging smile, he said to Randi, "You get to pick first. We usually hold it up above our heads and close our eyes so we don't pick all the favorites right away."

"That sounds like a good idea. What is your favorite?" Randi asked.

"Caramel."

She nodded. "I like that, too."

Gregory held the box for her and took off the lid. Cooperating with the game, she closed her eyes and reached up. When she did, she yelped and Gregory dropped the box. Tim and Sean giggled as Cade rose to his feet, rounded the table and stared at the mess on the floor—dirt but mostly worms. Worms that had given Randi a fright. Right now she was looking at them as if she'd like to make his sons eat them.

At the moment, Cade didn't think that was such a bad idea. It was time he put some fear into the three mischief-makers. He pointed to the stairs. "Up to your room. Now!" he thundered. "This time I might tan your hides."

His boys had never feared him. But hearing the deep anger vibrating in his voice now, their eyes grew wide and Sean's lower lip trembled. Even Gregory's usual stoic expression showed uncertainty and his eyes looked shiny.

Somehow Cade had to make them understand.

But before either he or the boys could take a step, Randi stood beside him, placing a restraining hand on his arm. "I'd like to handle this myself."

As much for his sons' benefit as hers, he said, "They need an iron hand now. I've been too lenient."

"Cade, please?"

Lord Almighty, those blue eyes could make the devil change his mind, let alone make him follow her anywhere. He gazed at his sons, at expressions that said they were afraid to go to their room and have him follow. He would never hit them. But apparently they didn't know that.

He rubbed the back of his neck. "Do whatever you want."

Randi heard the frustration and sorrow in Cade's voice. He was doing what he felt was right. She had no fear he would spank the boys; she realized he'd simply wanted to scare them. But she knew what fear could do, even something as seemingly innocuous as fear of a father's disapproval. It wasn't innocuous at all.

"Gregory, Tim, Sean. Let's go into the living room. I want to talk to you."

At the moment, they obviously saw her as a reprieve. She led the way and they followed.

The three of them sat together on the sofa. Cade stood in the archway.

Randi chose a chair across from them. "Why do you think I'm here?"

The three boys communicated silently with their eyes, and then Gregory acted as spokesperson. "Dad told us you're a guest, that you're just staying a little while. But we know better. You're our new housekeeper. We don't *want* a housekeeper.''

"Oh, so you don't believe what your dad tells you?"

Gregory's cheeks flushed; Sean and Tim directed their eyes to the floor.

"I *know* you don't want a housekeeper. Your dad told me you've treated them badly,'' she added. "And I think I understand why.''

Three pairs of eyes trained on her.

"You don't want a stranger coming into *your* house, telling *you* what to do.''

Little Sean nodded and Tim jabbed him in the ribs.

"Look, guys. I'm not your new housekeeper. I don't even know how long I'll be staying. I need a vacation from New York City. When I met your dad, he invited me to visit sometime. So here I am. But while I'm here, I offered to help him take care of you. It seemed a fair trade.''

Tim asked, "What did you do there?''

"I'm a lawyer.''

"Wow,'' Gregory murmured.

Randi glanced at Cade. The boys couldn't see their father, but she could. A small smile played on his lips. Before she got distracted by him, his tall masculine form casually canted against the door-jamb, she focused on the boys again. "I do like to bait a hook with worms and go fishing. I don't like to play with worms. I like to drink water and take showers with it, but I don't like to have it dumped on my head. Now, while I'm here, we can either learn to be friends, or you can pull pranks and we'll all probably be miserable. I'd really rather try to be friends. What do you think?''

None of the boys were quick to answer. That was good, as far as Randi was concerned, because they were thinking about what she'd said.

Suddenly Gregory looked at Cade, and the other two boys switched their attention to him, too.

He came into the center of the room. "Randi's right. I do need help. I can't run the ranch and take care of you the way I should without it.''

"But we've got Charlie!'' Gregory argued.

Cade went to the sofa and crouched down in front of his sons. "I know you like Charlie. But Charlie has his own jobs to do.''

The boys were frowning and silent.

Finally, Gregory looked at Randi. "Can you cook?''

"Some. But more importantly, I can read. So if you have favorite recipes or if we buy a cookbook, I shouldn't have too many problems.''

"Can we have somethin' else besides cereal for breakfast?'' Gregory asked.

"How about pancakes?'' Randi answered.

"We don't have time in the mornin' on school days," Tim complained.

"I get up early, guys. I'll make them. All you have to do is eat them."

"Mrs. Hunter *hated* to get up early," Tim said with a grin.

Cade stood. "So, gentlemen. Will you let Randi help me and not give her a rough time?"

Gregory looked at Tim.

Tim asked, "You really fish?"

"Sure do. I taught my two brothers."

Tim gave Gregory a nod. The oldest decided, "Okay. You can help. But you can't treat us like babies."

"I wouldn't think of it," Randi promised with an expression as serious as Gregory's.

"Sean?" Cade asked.

"I like pancakes," the four-year-old said enthusiastically. "Will you take care of me when Tim and Gregory's at school?"

"I suppose we can try that and give your dad and Charlie a chance to get their work done. Is that all right with you?"

Sean smiled and nodded.

With an answering smile that she hoped told the boys she appreciated their cooperation, she said, "If we help each other, we all benefit. Are you ready to help?"

The boys glanced at each other. Gregory asked suspiciously, "How?"

"While I clean up supper, Gregory, you could put the worms back where they belong. Tim, you could get the dustpan and brush to clean up the dirt. And Sean, it would be great if you helped me clear the table by throwing the napkins in the trash and collecting the silverware."

Cade chuckled when he saw his sons frown. "Remember, she'll make pancakes for breakfast."

The boys looked at their father, then at each other. Finally, Gregory answered for all of them. "We'll help."

Randi let out a pent-up breath. One hurdle crossed. Then she felt Cade's gaze on her. She had a feeling life on a ranch in Montana could be more exciting than her life in New York.

Restless and unable to sleep, Cade switched on his bedside lamp. Going to his window, he gazed out into black space, knowing he should feel relief. But he didn't. He was edgy. After supper, Randi had suggested a game of crazy eights. The boys had looked at her blankly. She'd asked for a deck of cards and shown them how to play.

Cade never played games with his sons. Oh, he wrestled with them, played pitch and catch, took them riding, but in the house for the evening, thanks to their satellite dish, they watched television or the videos he'd bought for their birthdays and Christmas. Cade's parents had never played games with him. And since he didn't have any brothers or sisters, he'd read or, as he grew, played sports. When Randi had asked his sons what card games they did know, Gregory and Tim had replied in unison, "Poker." Cade didn't have to ask where they'd learned that.

He went to his clothes chest and pulled out a pair of black sweatpants. Closing the door on the chest, he noticed his robe hanging on one bedpost. He remembered how Randi had looked in it as she'd scurried to her bedroom. He imagined how she'd look without it. Damn.

Not only was he attracted to her, but he liked her! Liking a woman. What a novel idea. Although he had to admit Jeff's new wife seemed nice enough. But Cade had been wary even of her.

His marriage to Susan had done that. Before they were married, he'd told her of his dream to one day buy into his uncle's ranch. He'd known it would take years until he had enough money saved. He didn't think it would matter because in the meantime, they would be building a life together. Susan had seemed happy enough after they were married. But after Gregory was born and Tim a year later, she'd changed. She became restless. The boys didn't seem to bring her the joy they did Cade. It was almost as if she resented having to care for them. He should have read the signs.

Because when she found out she was pregnant with Sean… Their youngest child's conception had been an accident, and Susan had blamed Cade for it. She blamed him most for not wanting her to abort the pregnancy. He couldn't imagine not fathering a life he'd created. And Susan…

Cade had thought she'd reconciled to the idea of another child. When his uncle had left him the ranch, she seemed to relish the idea of a move, even though she was five months pregnant. But apparently she'd thought she would be queen of a manor—like in the movies—rather than an ordinary wife and mother. In the months that followed, she'd been unable to reconcile herself to living on a ranch thirty miles from the nearest town. She'd hated the isolation. And shortly after Sean was born, she'd decided children and a husband would never be enough; they weren't even what she wanted. She'd gone back to her career as a fashion consultant. She'd gone back to New York.

It had taken Cade a year after her departure to admit he was as much to blame for the failure of their marriage as she was. He had expected too much. Because they'd exchanged vows, he'd thought they would share a life, no matter what it was. After Susan left, saying she'd married a stockbroker not a rancher who lived too far from civilization to remember what culture was, he'd felt betrayed in the deepest sense. He might have understood her abandoning their marriage, but he could never forgive her for abandoning their sons. The last he'd heard, she was traveling in Spain with her new husband, an investment banker.

The old memories increased Cade's edginess. Maybe a dish of ice cream would help him get to sleep. Hell, it was as good as anything else.

He pulled on the jogging pants and went downstairs. On the first floor, he saw a light on in the kitchen. Walking toward it, he stopped and stared.

Randi stood in front of the door, looking out, a glass of milk in hand. Her nightgown fell from her shoulders straight to her knees. The long sleeves were slightly full, the neckline round and low. Her hair flowed down her back and hid part of her face. The black night outside the door window defined her delicate profile—the straight, small nose, her softly pointed chin.

"Move away from the window," he growled as his body reacted to seeing her dressed in nightwear.

She turned toward him, and the overhead light in the kitchen gave her a glow that was almost ethereal. "There's no one around for miles. All the lights are out in the bunkhouse."

"That's because no one's *in* the bunkhouse. They should be back any time...."

Just as Cade finished speaking, a truck rattled

down the lane and pulled in. Cade crossed the kitchen, clasped her arm and pulled her to the side.

"Cade, I'm sorry. I'm very aware of that kind of thing in New York. Here—"

"Here, we still have men who are attracted to beautiful women. We may say 'ma'am' and 'thank you,' but that doesn't mean we don't want and need the same as any other men." His wants and needs were kicking him in the gut.

She looked at his hand on her arm, his bare chest, and finally his face. Cade saw the pulse at her throat quicken, the blue of her eyes become deeper. They could get into trouble and they both knew it.

He nodded to the glass of milk in her hand. "Have a problem sleeping?"

She licked her bottom lip before she answered. "I wasn't sure you approved of the way I handled your boys."

The sheen from her tongue remained on her lip. He couldn't imagine her any sexier if she stood before him naked. Releasing her arm, he stepped away and leaned against the counter. "I didn't thank you, did I?" After he'd put the boys to bed, he'd taken a shower. When he'd come downstairs again, Randi had already turned in. Or so he'd thought.

"I didn't know what you wanted me to do after they went to bed. We haven't discussed a plan of any kind."

He chuckled. "The organized sort. I knew it. What kind of plan did you have in mind?"

She didn't return his smile. "Do you want help putting the boys to bed or is that your special time with them? Do you want me to join the three of you after supper or do you want me to fade away? And after they're in bed, do you want me to occupy myself in my room?"

"You're not the type of woman to fade away." At her frown, he shrugged. "I haven't thought about it. Grace was part of the family. We liked it that way. Many nights she'd fall asleep on the sofa while I nodded off in the chair during the news. The housekeepers—they didn't seem to want to be involved. They went to their room after supper and there they stayed. You're not a housekeeper. You're a guest. So it depends on what you want to do. I suggest we take it one day at a time and just see what happens."

Randi looked perplexed for a moment, as if "one day at a time" was a new concept. "The boys have had to make a lot of adjustments," she said softly. The softness drifted over Cade, warming him, heating him.

He pulled open the freezer door and removed the tub of ice cream. Maybe if he concentrated on eating, he would forget that neither of them wore many clothes. "Yes, they have."

After a pause, Randi asked, "Do they ever talk about their mother?"

The question stabbed Cade so hard he almost dropped the ice cream. Then he turned around slowly, his jaw clenched.

Chapter Three

"No, they don't talk about their mother," Cade replied and clamped his jaw shut.

"Does she ever see them?"

"No."

Randi knew she was pushing. "Does she call or write?"

"No."

"Cade. I don't mean to pry. But it would help me to know the situation so I don't say or do anything to upset the boys."

He set the tub of ice cream on the table with a thump. "Susan deserted them and didn't look back."

Randi couldn't imagine a mother leaving her children or a man like Cade. "She deserted you, too," she said softly, more interested than she wanted to be in whether or not Cade still had feelings for his ex-wife.

He went perfectly still and pinned her with hard brown eyes. "I don't talk about Susan, either."

Randi could feel the anger emanating from him, the sense of betrayal that still seemed raw. "All right. I'll consider the subject off-limits."

His relief was obvious. His shoulders lost their rigidity as he turned to the drawer and took out an ice-cream scoop. When he took two dishes from the cupboard, he glanced over his shoulder at her. "Why did you leave New York?"

If he could stonewall her, she could stonewall him. "I don't want to discuss what happened before I left any more than you want to talk about your ex-wife."

He scooped the ice cream into the dishes and set them on the table. "It's not the same."

"How do you know?" she asked, annoyed he wasn't backing down as easily as she had.

"Because talking about Susan serves no useful purpose. But in your case, you'll be going back to whatever you left."

"I need time and distance."

"To do what?"

Already, she suspected Cade could be hard and relentless if he chose. But she wouldn't let him intimidate her. "I need to think, Cade, about the

choices I've made, the career I've chosen, the influ-
ence my father has had on my life. I need to think
about all of it and then decide what *I* want—not to
compete with my brothers or make my father proud,
but because what I choose will make me happy."

Cade's surprise lifted his brows. "That's a mouth-
ful. Something mighty serious must have happened
to send you running."

"I'm not running," she protested. "And if you're
suggesting I'm a coward for leaving—"

The ice cream forgotten, he came toward her
slowly. "Whoa, there." Lifting a lock of her auburn
hair, he smiled. "It doesn't take much to get you
riled, does it?"

As he brushed his thumb over her hair, she imagined how his touch would feel on her skin. With as
much poise as she could muster, she answered, "Actually, it does."

He arched an eyebrow. "But I'm the exception?"

"You and my brothers. They know the buttons to
push. You…just push."

He chuckled. "You're a rare breed, Randi. An
honest woman."

The sound of his amusement was deep and masculine, triggering the urge to step closer to him. But
she knew that would be dangerous. You didn't tempt
a man like Cade without planning to follow through.
"Not so rare."

Cade's gaze lingered on the lock of hair between

his fingers, then moved to her face. It stopped on her lips. She read the desire in his eyes and felt an answering response, a response that was as foreign in its intensity as it was in its being there at all. Cade stirred something so deep, she didn't know where it came from.

He leaned toward her and she held her breath, but shadows clouded his eyes and he stepped away. Randi had to admit she was relieved. If he kissed her, then what? If he kissed her, what could happen with three tornadoes swirling around them? If he kissed her, something might start that neither of them was ready to deal with. In fact, sitting here, eating ice cream with him in the middle of the night, trying to pretend the tension humming between them had nothing to do with her nightgown and his bare chest would be impossible.

Running her hand through her hair, she lifted it away from her face. His gaze followed the movement of her hand, and the nerve in his jaw worked. She ignored the sheer bulk of him, the magnetic pull toward him, and said, "I'd better get to bed. Something tells me I'll need lots of energy for tomorrow. Are the boys up at sunrise?"

"Soon after."

She crossed to the doorway. "I'll see you in the morning."

He just nodded.

She got away while she could.

* * *

Cade stood at the kitchen window, nursing his second cup of coffee. He knew he'd narrowly escaped disaster last night. The two dishes of ice cream had done nothing to cool his desire or make him forget about wanting to kiss Randi. He didn't know what was wrong with him. Since Susan had left, turning away from women hadn't been a problem. He'd just remind himself of the betrayal, the heartache, and most of all his three sons, and desire had faded into oblivion. But ever since he'd seen Randi at the wedding...

When he heard footsteps, he took another long sip of coffee, then slowly turned.

She looked about sixteen in her white sweater and gray jeans, her ponytail hanging over one shoulder. With an uncertain expression, she stood in the archway to the kitchen. "I'm sorry I overslept."

"You were up late. And yesterday was a full day. Traveling itself is tiring, let alone dealing with Tim, Sean and Gregory. Would you like some breakfast? There are five kinds of cereal...."

She nodded toward the counter. "Coffee's fine. I usually skip breakfast."

"Breakfast is the most important meal of the day," he said mechanically as if repeating it to his sons.

She smiled. "I think I've heard that somewhere before."

As she crossed to the coffeepot, her ponytail

swung across her back. The tendrils waved and rippled when she walked. He'd like to slip his fingers through it, hold her steady, and—

"Where are the boys?"

"Bothering Charlie. I told him I'd like some time to show you around. He said he'd occupy them."

"You don't have to entertain me. And if I can do something useful like helping with the boys, I will. I don't want to feel like a guest."

A guest. He'd rather she stayed a guest, but that wasn't going to happen. She was too good with his sons and he could use her help until he found someone permanent. "Showing you around isn't entertaining. It'll help you get your bearings and learn what goes on, what the boys are liable to get into."

She poured herself a cup of coffee and added milk from the carton on the counter. Then she automatically tucked it on the shelf where it belonged in the refrigerator. She took a few sips, then eyed him over the rim. "What do you usually do on Sundays?"

"Odds and ends. Spend some time with the boys if no emergencies crop up. I thought maybe we'd have a picnic for lunch. Before you know it, winter will set in."

"But it's only the end of September."

"The snow falls in October sometimes. I hope it holds off this year until we're ready for it. We have a lot of ground to cover before then."

After a few more sips of coffee, she set her cup on the table. "Okay, I'm ready."

He hoped to hell he was and opened the door for her.

As soon as they neared the corral, two cowhands on horses stared at Randi. When she smiled, they tipped their hats.

Cade introduced her. "Al, Buck, this is Miranda Sinclair. She'll be staying at the ranch—" He hesitated, then continued, "A few weeks."

Not to be daunted by Stetsons and boots rather than suits and ties, she said, "It's nice to meet you."

Al and Buck stared at her as if she were from another planet and looked uncomfortable. Finally, Buck said, "We're gonna ride out to South Ridge and check the calves."

Cade nodded. "I'm going to show Randi around. Have you seen Charlie and the boys?"

Buck smiled. "They're 'helping' him repair the tractor." With a last tip of their hat brims, the two men rode out.

Randi frowned as she and Cade walked to the barn.

"What's wrong?"

She glanced over her shoulder. "They were looking at me as if I had two noses."

Cade laughed. "Your reputation preceded you. I'm sure Charlie told them about everything from the bucket to the worms."

"And?" she pressed.

Her hair glowed with red fire in the morning sun. Her blue eyes rivaled the color of the sky. For a moment he forgot what he'd been about to say. A breeze brought the sweet scent of her to him, and he realized she could too easily distract him and make him search for lost dreams. That was a wild-goose chase he wouldn't attempt again.

Remembering the topic of their conversation, he said, "You look about sixteen and they were probably wondering how you hog-tied Gregory, Tim and Sean."

"I didn't hog-tie them. I *talked* to them."

Cade shook his head. "Yeah, well, I *talk* to them, too. And it usually lasts a few hours. So if they offer you candy again after lunch, don't expect chocolates."

Randi stepped through the barn door, knowing Cade was right. She might have passed some kind of initiation, but that didn't mean his sons would listen to her on a regular basis.

The smell of horses, leather and hay wound about her as she walked down the aisle between the stalls. She stopped when she came to a lovely bay. The horse's soft brown eyes met hers and she smiled, stepping closer. "Hi, there, girl. Aren't you a pretty one."

"Smart and quick, too. Summer is Gregory's, but

I talked to him earlier and he said you can ride her. Do you ride?"

"I used to. English not Western. I rode in competitions when I was a teenager."

"I should have guessed," he mumbled.

"I think I hear some disapproval."

Cade shrugged, the motion making his shoulders seem even broader in the denim work shirt. "There's a big difference between riding for show and riding for work or to actually cover ground."

"Yes, I guess there is. But whether you're in Montana or upstate New York, nothing can compare to the feel of a wonderful animal under you and the wind in your face. I think riding is the closest I'll ever come to knowing how a bird feels soaring through the sky."

"It sounds as if you're ready to try it again."

She nodded. "Could be."

Cade was looking at her strangely—as if he was trying to figure her out. She didn't know what had gotten into her since she'd stepped off the plane in Billings. A sense of adventure, maybe? Whatever it was, she was going to make the most of it while she was here. She'd felt stifled for too long.

Leaving the bay, she stopped in front of a beautiful black gelding. The horse threw back its head and neighed, giving her a wary stare.

"This is Storm. He's mine." There was pride in Cade's voice and the respect a man gives an animal he depends upon. He offered his hand to the animal and the horse nuzzled his master's palm. They looked right together—strong, solid, a team.

Cade said to her, "Come here. Stand beside me."

Moving closer to him, she was too aware of Cade's height, his scent, his virility and the power it carried with it.

"Just lay your hand on the stall."

She rested her hand on the top board. Cade laid his next to hers. The contrast was startling. His hand was bronze, large, weathered. Hers seemed fragile, pale, as if it hadn't seen the sun this season. She trembled and they weren't even touching. Why did he affect her so?

Storm lifted his head and stretched his neck. First he brushed Cade's fingers, then he nudged hers.

"Hold still," Cade murmured, although it was an order. Usually Randi balked against dictums for their own sake, but she suspected Cade had a purpose. A moment later, he said, "He's shy of strangers."

Like his master? she wondered.

"Go ahead. You can stroke him now."

Randi fondled the horse's nose, loving the softness and the warmth.

"You have a nice touch," Cade said in a low tone.

Casting him a sideways glance, she got caught by the golden sparks there. They warmed up the barn and made Cade seem even closer than he was.

Tired of the attention, Storm turned to his feed trough and ignored them. Cade chuckled. "That's what I like about horses. They know when they've had enough." His gaze ran over Randi from her ponytail to her sneakers. "Did you bring boots?"

"Yes."

"I'll saddle up the horses. You go get the boots. You'd better grab a jacket, too."

"Cade, if you have other things you'd rather do…"

"I don't. It's been a while since I took a ride for the sheer pleasure of it. You reminded me of that."

She saw him disappear into the tack room as she headed back to the house. There was always a purpose about Cade. He didn't move or talk without good reason.

When she entered the kitchen, Charlie was standing at the sink; the boys were drinking glasses of milk.

With a milk mustache surrounding his mouth, Sean said, "You got a message on the machine."

Tim nodded. "It's a *long* one. We listened."

Charlie flushed sheepishly. "Sorry about that. It's an event around here when that little red light's blinkin'."

"It was your dad," Gregory added with a solemn look.

Randi's heart beat faster. "Then I guess I'd better listen to it."

Gregory pointed to the living room. "It's in there. C'mon, I'll show you how to get it." In the living room, he went to the table by the sofa and pressed the button on the machine. "We rewound it already."

As her father's voice blared out clear and vehement, Randi clenched her hands.

"Miranda, I know you're there. My private investigator found you. If you're trying to hide, you didn't cover your tracks very well. David is as upset as you are. He couldn't tell you the truth. You wouldn't have defended Johnson. This is nothing to jeopardize your career over or your relationship with David. Call me. Immediately."

Randi stared at the machine as it clicked off.

Gregory said, "He sounds mad."

She brought her attention to the little boy. "He always sounds mad."

"Even when you don't do nothin' wrong?"

She tried to smile. "He thinks I do lots of things wrong."

Gregory stared at her for a long moment. "That's tough."

She nodded. "Yep, it is sometimes."

"You gonna call him?"

She shook her head. "Not now. I'm going riding with your dad."

"Yeah, he said he might take you. If you know how. Do you?"

"It's been a long time, but I think it'll come back."

"Summer's easy."

She studied the eight-year-old's expression.

"You don't mind if I ride her?"

He shook his head again.

Randi tried to put her father's voice out of her mind as she yanked on her boots and grabbed her jacket. But she could still hear the disapproval.

When she came downstairs, Charlie and the boys were gone. Once outside, she saw them by the barn talking to Cade. At least Charlie was talking to Cade. Gregory, Tim and Sean were playing tag.

Cade held Summer's reins as Randi hoisted herself into the saddle. The leather creaked and she held on to the horn while she got her bearings.

Cade asked, "Are you ready?"

She took the reins and patted Summer's neck. "I'm ready."

After they waved to Charlie and the boys, Cade led her along a packed-earth trail. After a quarter of a mile, he pointed north across the grassland. She followed him at a trot, feeling as if she would bounce out of the saddle. She was used to posting and hugging the saddle and horse with her knees. She felt much less in control with this bulkier seat. Although she imagined she could bounce off any minute, Cade couldn't look more comfortable. His back was straight, although his posture was relaxed.

He held the reins in one hand, his other hand resting on his thigh. With his black Stetson low on his forehead, he was the picture of every cowboy who'd ever ridden the range. Yet, Cade could never be one of many. His bearing and confidence would always make him stand out.

It seemed as if they rode forever, through grass, with cattle grazing at the foot of cottonwoods, toward blue sky that seemed never ending. Eventually, catching on to Summer's rhythm, Randi relaxed and became part of the motion. The breeze tugged strands of her hair from her ponytail.

Cade slowed Storm to a walk as they approached the bank of a creek. She did the same, raising her face to the sun, relishing the sense of freedom that sang through the air. Wide-open spaces, few boundaries, fresh clean air that filled her lungs, energizing her. How could anyone *not* love this country?

Cade attached Storm's reins to some brush and stood beside Summer, ready to help Randi dismount.

"I'm okay," she assured him as she swung her leg over and slid to the grass. But as soon as her feet touched the ground, her knees almost buckled.

Cade held her by the elbows. With his chin almost resting on the crown of her head, his tall body supporting hers, not only her legs felt weak. "It's been a long time," he murmured.

She *knew* he was talking about her last riding jaunt, but his low, husky voice, the clasp of his hands on her arms, and his words brushing her temple created a picture of a bedroom, dim lights... Taking a deep breath she composed herself and willed her legs to stop quivering.

She turned, which was no easy feat with him standing so close. "I'm fine." He took a step away, and she latched on to the saddle for balance.

As she stomped on one foot then the other, her leg muscles remembered what they were supposed to do.

"*Are* you fine, Randi? Charlie told me about the phone call."

Stepping away from Summer, Randi looked toward the creek. "I've been dealing with my father all my life."

"Did you call him back?"

"No. I'm too angry and hurt and disappointed. He knew the man I was defending was guilty. He *knew* that David knew Johnson was guilty. And David—"

Suddenly Cade was clasping her shoulder. "Start at the beginning."

She shook her head. "It's too long a story."

With gentle pressure, he turned her toward him. "I've got time."

It was odd, really. Cade had a ranch to run that took long, grueling hours. He'd told her himself he never felt caught up. He also had three sons who required love and plenty of attention. Yet, looking into his steady brown eyes, she believed him when he said he had time to listen. Still, she hesitated.

"I won't make any judgments, Randi."

She was used to judgments. "My mom and I were close. When she died, I was ten, my brothers were eight and seven. I felt responsible for them. I felt as if I had to take care of them. Dad hired a housekeeper, but she didn't handle scraped knees and missing Mom in the middle of the night."

"And your father?"

"My father basically ignored me. Maybe he didn't know what to do with me after Mom died. When he was around, he praised my brothers' accomplishments, whether it was sports or schoolwork. I became a lawyer to try to get his attention. To show him he could be proud of me, too. The problem was—he's a corporate attorney and I found that branch of the law dull. I wanted to help people."

"Your father didn't find that admirable?"

"My father thought I was foolish working for a legal-aid clinic in D.C. after I passed the bar. So when a New York City law firm approached me, I accepted their offer. I think it was the first time in my life my dad approved of something I did."

"What happened?"

She gazed across the creek, up into the clouds that had gathered in snowy white bunches. "I earned a reputation for believing in my clients. Other lawyers knew it. Judges knew it. When Dad introduced me to David, David knew it.''

"You and this David. You got involved?"

The edge to Cade's voice brought her gaze back to his. "We dated. After a few dates, he asked if I'd consider representing a friend of his who'd gotten into some trouble through no fault of his own. That's what David said and I believed him. I also believed the man when I took him on as a client.''

"He used you," Cade remarked.

"*Used* is too kind a word. I received a call from the D.A. He had irrefutable proof my client was guilty of fraud, amongst other counts. He urged us to cut a deal. I cut the deal, reassigned my cases, and then I cut out. I had so many questions and self-doubts. How could I have misjudged two men so? Had David's charm blinded me so I couldn't see his true character? Or had my father's approval meant so much I'd fooled myself about David? I prided myself on being such a good judge of character, yet I couldn't even see through my client. What kind of woman am I? What kind of lawyer? What's happened to my logic and good sense? Can I believe anything my father ever tells me again?''

"He admitted he knew?"

"He not only admitted he knew. He wants me to get back together with David because he's a rising star in advertising and he can enhance my reputation, introduce me to the right people—'' Her voice broke and the emotions of the last week finally caught up to her. She stared at Cade's chest and blinked away the tears that suddenly materialized.

"I understand betrayal, Randi." He raised her chin with his thumb.

There was something about this man that was so strong and so sturdy. "How do you stop the questions? How do you ever trust your instincts again?"

He frowned. "I said I understand. I didn't say I have the answers." His large hand still clasped her shoulder. His hat cast a shadow over his features, but it didn't soften the thrust of his jaw or diminish the character lines etched around his eyes. How could a woman desert a man like this, full of strength and caring and honesty that had Randi almost believing she could trust again?

"You're a good listener."

He stayed silent.

She went on quickly. "I didn't mean to dump on you. I'm used to handling my problems myself. But I guess my father's call just made it a little overwhelming."

"Don't apologize, Randi."

"I'm not. But I don't do this—"

He slid his finger over her lips and effectively cut off her words. "I've told my sons and I'm telling you. There's nothing wrong with tears if there's a good reason for them. You've got a good reason."

The touch of his skin on her lips was exciting. But what was even more exciting was the darkening of his brown gaze and the quickening of his breath. It matched hers. When he bent his head, she closed her eyes.

From the moment his lips touched hers, her senses reeled. The scents of Cade and autumn in Montana surrounded her, along with his arms. His strength, the heat of him, was as arousing as the pressure of his mouth. Without letting herself think about the consequences, she leaned into him and curled her hands on his shoulders. Holding on seemed more a necessity now than when she'd bounced on Summer.

He held her loosely, but when his tongue singed the seam of her lips, she felt his palms press into her back. Her heart thudded. No man had ever waited for her like this. No man had ever made her heart pound so hard it drowned out the voice of caution. She parted her lips, inviting him to taste her.

Cade tried to sort his thoughts, but gave up. The feel of Randi in his arms, the sweet scent of her, her soft womanly curves tight against him, drove him to satisfy a need rather than think about his actions. If he didn't know better, he would have thought his herd was stampeding through his head; but experience told him it was the sound of his heart.

When Randi parted her lips, he realized just how long he'd been denying needs that he'd told himself had taken a vacation. They were back, raring to go, ready to lead him to more than a kiss. Yet the kiss was so hot, so tempting, so gloriously arousing in itself. He couldn't remember a kiss ever being quite like this. He couldn't remember needing and wanting so much after a simple brush of lips, the easy stroke of his tongue.

Randi's taste was as sweet as her smell. He stroked again and again, eager for a response from her. Finally, she curved her fingers into his shoulders, the action signaling her arousal. She met his forays with sweeps of her own, and Cade realized he wouldn't care if the kiss lasted forever. He passed his hands up and down her back. She felt so fragile. Yet he knew instinctively she wasn't. She'd already proved with his sons that she was made of stern stuff. And after what she'd been through—

Been through. David. New York. What in hell's bells was he doing kissing her like this when she could have a man waiting for her, when she had a *life* waiting for her? Hadn't he learned his lesson with Susan? A woman didn't belong out here. Oh, sure, in summer and fall the scenery couldn't be matched anywhere. But when the winter winds blew and the snow fell...

He tore away before he couldn't. He tore away because of a failed marriage and smashed dreams. He tore away because Miranda Sinclair was a woman of refinement—educated and city bred. She would never be happy here. She would never stay. Acknowledging the kiss and the passion they'd stirred up could only make the situation worse.

"Cade?"

Her wide blue eyes and gentle voice played over

him like a soft summer wind. "It never happened,"
he said almost harshly.

She blinked. "Excuse me?"

"We're living under the same roof, Miranda, and
if you want to stay, that can't happen again. I've got
enough on my plate."

Her expression changed from desire-dazed to
thoroughly annoyed. "You have enough on *your*
plate? It seems to me *you're* the one who started
whatever happened," she finished.

His cheeks darkened. "Maybe so. But you wanted
it, too."

"*I'm* not denying it," she retorted.

"No, but you'd better. I haven't been with a
woman for a long time, Miranda. I don't want to use
you or take advantage of a situation that can only
bring us both grief. So, as far as I'm concerned, I'm
going to forget what just happened."

She studied him and then said, "Fine. I'll pretend
it never happened. But I won't forget it, Cade. I'm
more honest with myself than that." She swung
around and headed for Summer.

Cade swore and stared at her ponytail swinging
across her back. It was better this way. Distance was
safer.

He *had* learned his lesson. He could resist temptation and one pretty lawyer from New York. How
hard could it be?

Chapter Four

Randi offered to groom Summer, but Cade brushed her offer aside. When she went into the house, Charlie and the boys were packing a large wicker picnic basket. Gregory asked, "Did you like Summer?"

Randi shed her jacket and hung it on one of the higher pegs behind the door. "She's a wonderful horse. Thank you for letting me ride her."

There must have been something amiss in her voice because Charlie narrowed his eyes and examined her closely. "We're about ready here. Cade takin' care of the horses?"

She nodded and realized Cade's second kiss had shaken her much more than his first. But shaken or not, there was something she had to do. "I'm going to make a phone call."

Charlie lifted the basket. "C'mon, boys. Let's give Miss Sinclair some privacy." Shooing Cade's sons toward the door, he added, "Come around back when you're finished. But don't take too long or it might be all gone." With a wink, he closed the door behind them.

Taking a deep breath, Randi went to the living room, picked up the phone, and dialed her father's number. He picked up on the first ring.

"Hello, Dad."

"Come back to New York."

"No, I need a vacation and I'm taking it."

"You're running away like a whipped dog. So you lost this one. It happens."

"This isn't about losing," she said sadly.

"Life's always about winning and losing. Haven't you learned that yet?"

"Apparently not. I'm not upset because Johnson will be going to prison. He deserves that. He committed a crime."

"On paper. It's not as if—"

"Dad, listen to yourself. He defrauded stockholders. He lied and cheated."

"Grow up, Miranda. Take off the rose-colored glasses. You can't put your career in jeopardy over this."

"My career's not in jeopardy, just my peace of mind. When I'm ready, I'll come back to New York and not a moment before. So just cut out the intimidation tactics. Your approval or disapproval carries no weight anymore.''

"You are a stubborn woman, Miranda. David is waiting.…''

"I told David exactly where he could go before I left. Forget it, Dad. David and I never really worked and now I know why. He didn't care about me. If he had, he wouldn't have set out to use me.''

"You don't realize what you're doing.''

"I realize exactly what I'm doing. I'm licking my wounds and breathing fresh air. Goodbye, Dad. I'll let you know when I get back.'' Then she hung up.

Suddenly, she smiled. She'd stood up to him. The sky hadn't caved in. Her world hadn't fallen apart. As a matter of fact, it felt a whole lot more steady. Going into the kitchen, she took her jacket from its peg. If she could stand up to her father, she could stand up to one sexy cowboy who knew how to kiss better than… Well, she didn't know what else he was good at, but she was going to find out. Then she'd make him realize that forgetting their kiss wouldn't be as easy as opening his eyes and blinking it away.

When she rounded the corner of the house, Charlie was tumbling Sean upside down through his arms. Cade and Tim were spreading a second blanket under a cottonwood. She stopped at the edge of the first. Gregory was already digging inside the basket.

She sat on a corner, cross-legged. "What are we having?"

"Peanut butter and ham."

"Together?"

He giggled. "No, *I* like peanut butter." He pointed to his brothers. "*They* like ham."

"Would you like me to cook supper tonight?" she called to Cade.

Finally, he met her gaze. "That's up to you."

She was sure Charlie and the boys would be able to feel the tension zipping between them. She didn't look away first. She wouldn't forget a kiss that had rocked her from head to toe just because it had been a foolish impulse on both their parts.

Charlie tickled Sean and called back, "If you can't find anything in the house that suits, come out to the freezer in the bunkhouse."

With a sandwich in one hand and a carrot in the other, Gregory sidled up next to her on the blanket and murmured, "Did you call?"

This eight-year-old wasn't just a rascal with mischief on his mind and she knew immediately what he meant. "Yes, I did."

When Gregory kept looking at her expectantly, she had to smile. "It was okay, Gregory. He wasn't happy with me, but I'm used to that."

Cade's oldest son lowered his voice to almost a whisper. "When Dad gets mad, he doesn't stay mad. Except at our mother. He's always mad about her."

Now *that* was a conversation Randi would like to explore. But she wouldn't pump Gregory for information. And with everyone else not so far away, it wasn't a good idea, anyway. Still, she wanted Gregory to know he was free to talk about his mother if he felt like it. "I bet you miss her."

"I don't remember her much."

She would love to put her arms around this little boy and give him a huge hug, but it was too soon for that. "Do you have a picture?"

Gregory shook his head. "Dad burned them."

Randi glanced up at Cade. He was watching her and Gregory speculatively, although he couldn't hear what they were saying. She could sense the anger he still carried toward his ex-wife, and the bitterness. He might have tried to keep it from touching his sons, but the spillover was still there.

As they ate lunch on the blankets, Charlie said to Cade, "I should go help Buck and Al repair fence."

"Better yet, you could enter last month's figures into the computer. I just haven't had the time."

Randi guessed there were no days off on a ranch. "Boys, how would you like to bake cookies with me this afternoon?"

"What kind?" Sean asked.

She was learning he was the practical one. "We could try chocolate chip if you have the ingredients."

"We don't got no chocolate chips," Charlie remarked. "Got some chocolate bars at the bunkhouse, though."

Randi nodded. "And if I can't find a recipe, I'll call Katie."

"Grace left her cookbooks." Cade took another sandwich from the picnic basket. "Are you sure you want to spend this afternoon cooped up in the kitchen?"

She could read the underlying question. *Did she want to handle his boys for the afternoon?* "I haven't had time to putter in the kitchen since I was home with my brothers." She winked at his sons. "With three helpers it should be fun. I'm sure they can show me where everything is."

Cade suppressed a smile. "I'm sure they can." He pointed at Tim. "No sand."

Tim shook his head and looked sheepish.

As daylight dwindled, Cade strode to the house, not knowing what he'd find. He half expected Randi to be tied up on a kitchen chair, his renegades doing a war dance around her. On the other hand, as well as she'd managed the situation last night, she might be supervising while *they* made supper. He had to smile. But then he remembered the feel of her lips on his, her softness, his arousal, and his smile faded.

Forget the kiss, he reminded himself as he opened the door.

The myriad aromas hit him first—roasting beef,

steamed vegetables, chocolate and the wholesome smell of baking. As he took in the scene before him, his gut twisted because it resembled so exactly the picture he'd had in his head when he'd moved to the ranch; a picture of his dream. Randi stood at the stove stirring gravy, her cheeks flushed from the oven's heat. Sean stood on a kitchen chair beside her, watching. Gregory was scooping coffee into the coffeepot. Tim was placing silverware beside each plate that lay on the blue-and-white checked tablecloth. How long had it been since a tablecloth covered the table?

And to top it off, dried flowers of some kind sat in a glass in the center of the table. He swallowed hard.

"Hey, Dad," Tim called. "Better get washed up. Randi says supper's almost ready."

Cade closed the door and shrugged out of his jacket, hanging it on one of the high pegs. Then he took off his hat and ran his hand through his hair. "Do I have five minutes for a shower?"

Randi turned and smiled at him. "Take ten. We have to mash the potatoes yet."

Cade couldn't make himself head straight for the stairs. Crossing to Sean, he slung his arm around his son's shoulders. "What are you doing?"

"I'm watchin' it bubble. When it bubbles, it's gravy!"

His gaze met Randi's above Sean's head. "I don't see any lumps."

She laughed. "Should we put a few in?"

He chuckled. "No, thanks."

Gregory brought the coffeepot to Randi. She put it on the back burner and turned it on.

Cade ruffled Sean's hair. "I'll be back in a flash."

As Cade showered, he saw the scene in the kitchen again in his mind's eye. Then he frowned. The meal wasn't an everyday occurrence. Randi would get tired of playing housekeeper and she'd be gone. They'd go back to lumpy gravy and a table without a cloth or flowers. *So enjoy it while you can,* he told himself. *But don't get used to it.*

Dinner tasted every bit as good as it smelled. And when Gregory proudly placed a dish of chocolate-chip cookies on the table and Randi poured the coffee, Cade took a deep breath and reminded himself again that the moment was fleeting.

After the boys finished their cookies, they got antsy in their chairs. Finally Gregory asked, "Do we hafta clean up?"

Randi smiled. "You were such a big help making supper, I don't think you have to clean up."

The boys scrambled from their chairs.

Tim asked, "Can we play cards again tonight?"

Cade glanced at Randi and she shrugged. "I suppose we can. You can play in your room if you want till we finish here."

Quicker than lightning, the three of them ran up the stairs.

Randi stood and when she did, she winced.

"Uh-oh. Your muscles are telling you you were riding for the first time in a long time. You'd better get a hot bath before you turn in."

She began clearing the table. "I didn't think I was that out of shape." As she crossed to the sink, she glanced at him over her shoulder. "Can I ask you something?"

"If you're asking me before you ask, it means I might not want to answer. But you can ask." He took another sip of coffee from his mug and waited.

"Do you have any pictures of Susan?"

Damn it, why couldn't she leave the subject alone?

"I think Gregory would like to have one," she added quietly.

"And just why do you think that?" Cade snapped, keeping a rein on his temper.

"Something he said."

"Gregory never talks about his mother."

"Because of you."

"Now wait a minute." Cade pushed his chair back, the wooden legs scraping on the tile. "I never said they couldn't talk about their mother."

Randi opened the bottom cupboard and took out the dishwashing detergent. "You don't have to say it. They can sense your attitude. Even more, they can sense your anger.''

"I'm *not* angry. She's gone. She's forgotten."

"I can hear it in your voice and so can they. There's nothing wrong with being angry at her, Cade. She deserves your anger for deserting her family. But Gregory misses not having a mother. He said you burned all her pictures. Is that true?''

Cade felt as if somebody had slammed him in the gut with a two-by-four. "How the hell did he know that?"

The compassion in Randi's eyes carried almost as much impact as her words. "I don't know."

"That night after she left, I was so…" The slice of pain was as real as it had been that night. He spun away from Randi and stared out the door window. "After I put the boys to bed, I took the photo album out back. One by one I tore the pictures into the trash barrel. And then I lit it."

"Could Gregory have followed you?"

"He might have been able to see from his bedroom window." Cade stuffed his hands into his pockets. Why hadn't Gregory come to him about this? Randi had been here one day and already she'd stirred up his hormones and a hornet's nest about Susan. "Did you ask Gregory about his mother?"

Randi looked shocked. "Of course not!"

He stared her down, looking for a flicker of deception in her blue eyes. "Then how did the subject come up?"

"It just did, Cade. If you were more open about your feelings, Tim and Sean might want to talk about her, too."

"Don't you sound just like a woman. 'Open about my feelings.' Stay out of it, Randi. Don't go stirring something up you can't finish. With me...or the boys."

She looked hurt—but only for an instant. She quickly masked it. "I'm your guest, Cade, so I'll try to abide by your wishes. But if your sons want to talk to me, I won't turn them away. I know firsthand how it feels when an adult does that to a child." With that, she plopped the dishes into the sink and turned the water on fast.

Randi had capitulated to him, but it didn't feel like a victory. As a matter of fact, Cade felt as if he'd lost big-time.

Cade's sons had fun playing cards. Randi joked with them and teased them, eliciting smiles and giggles. When it was time to tuck the boys in, she said politely, "If you don't mind, I'll get my bath now."

He hated the formality of her tone, the niggling voice inside his head that told him he'd insulted her when she was only trying to help. "If you need a fresh towel..."

"No, I don't. What time do you want breakfast tomorrow?"

"I usually get the boys up at six-thirty. They're ready to eat by seven and the bus comes at seven-thirty. But if you'd rather sleep in, feel free."

"I said I'd help and I will. Good night, Cade." And with that, she climbed the steps. Her robe dangled over her arm and brushed the banister as she walked up.

After he put his sons to bed, Cade paced the living room. Then he went to the kitchen and opened the cupboards. Charlie would be going into Hampton tomorrow for supplies. It was time to stock up for winter.

Cade was still working on the list when he heard the steps creak. If he knew what was good for him, he'd stay put. Randi had already said good-night. He glanced at the list. But she might want Charlie to pick up something particular in town. He really should ask.

She'd reached the landing when he stopped in the archway. All he could do was stare. The satin robe she wore was pale green and revealed a lot more of her curves than *his* bulky terry-cloth robe. And his body responded accordingly.

She stopped still for a moment, then came down the remaining steps.

He couldn't resist the pull toward her, and he met her at the bottom. "Charlie's going into town tomorrow for supplies. I'm making a list. Do you have anything to add?"

She held her jeans and sweater more tightly in front of her. "Maybe I could go along. Do you think he'd mind?"

"I can ask him."

His gaze drifted to the V of her robe, the swell of her breasts. "I didn't mean to jump on you earlier." She stood silent, and he felt even more uncomfortable. "It's just that the boys and I have managed just fine for the past three years without any interference."

When she still didn't respond, he said, "Aren't you going to say anything?"

She started to move past him. "Good night, Cade."

He clasped her arm. "Say what you're thinking." The scent of the soap he usually bought smelled a hell of a lot different on her than on him. It was provocative and urged him to draw her closer and inhale deeper.

"You'll only get angry again, Cade. I think I'll keep my opinion to myself, thank you."

"Don't go all cold and icy on me, Randi. You're not like that."

She looked at his hand on her arm, then asked softly, "What do you want from me?"

Removing his hand, but wishing he didn't have to, he muttered, "Damned if I know. But I don't want you biting your tongue when something's clearly on your mind."

When she tilted her head, her hair spilled over her shoulder, thick and vibrant and full of fire. "All right. I think your boys have taken their cue from you. They don't talk about their mother but I think they need to. Did you ever tell them her leaving wasn't their fault? Did you ever tell them she'll always be their mother no matter what happens? Ten years from now, she might want to have a relationship with them."

"She doesn't have the right."

"No, but they do. You have to leave the door open for their sake. And you can't go on pretending she never existed. That's not good for them."

"So you think you have all the answers." After all, *he* was the parent; *he* was the one who had raised his sons thus far and done a pretty good job. They were good kids. They usually listened and obeyed— except when it came to housekeepers they didn't like.

Randi shook her head at his words. "I don't have the answers. I only know that as a child I wondered if my mother's death had anything to do with me. I wondered if I could have done something differently or said something differently to prevent it from happening. Children blame themselves for everything that goes wrong around them."

Cade thought about his own parents who lived in northern Pennsylvania. They'd given him a secure home, more love than he could ever imagine. Fortunately, they were still healthy, working, saving for a retirement they could enjoy together. He hadn't known loss till his uncle died. That had been hard. But Susan's leaving had been devastating. He'd thought the best thing to do for his sons was to go on as normally as they could. And they'd done fine until Grace left. Hadn't they?

Yet, why would Gregory talk to Randi about his mother unless she was still important to him? He was the oldest. He would remember her the most.

"I thought pretending Susan never existed would hurt them less. Maybe I was wrong." He couldn't resist the understanding in Randi's blue eyes, and he took a step closer to her.

She looked up at him, her lips slightly parted, her breathing quickening.

But he didn't touch her. If he did, they'd kiss and maybe a lot more. Instead he said, "You'd better go to your room before *I* stir something up."

He saw her deep intake of breath, the nod of her head that acknowledged the wisdom of his conclusion. Stepping away from him, she murmured, "I'll see you in the morning."

He watched her go to the doorway of her room, step inside, and close the door, not feeling very wise at all.

The muscles from Randi's waist to her knees protested as she vigorously stirred the pancake batter.

Grace's cookbooks listed most basic recipes with easy-to-follow directions. Randi wished she had easy-to-follow directions for dealing with Cade.

She'd heard him get up and leave the house at four-thirty, then come back in at six-thirty. Now, he was upstairs helping the boys get ready for school. She would have offered to help but decided it would be better if he asked. After yesterday, she didn't want to set foot where she wasn't wanted.

By the time Cade and the boys came downstairs, she'd set the platter of pancakes on the table. "Get 'em while they're hot."

"Oh, boy! She really *does* know how to make pancakes," Sean said as he slid onto his chair.

Randi sat, too, and winced when she did.

Cade disappeared for a moment and returned with a pillow. "Here. This will help. You should feel better tomorrow."

He was standing beside her, towering over her. Taking the pillow, she slid it under her.

Cade watched, amusement dancing in his eyes. "If you still want to go into town with Charlie, he says it's fine with him. You could tell him to take it easy on the bumps."

As Cade went back to his chair and sat, she asked, "What time should I plan supper?"

"Around seven should be good. I like the boys to finish their homework before we eat. Don't let them tell you they don't have any."

''Are you going to meet us at the bus stop?'' Tim asked.

''Usually one of the hands or I meet them down at the road. If you could do it, I'd appreciate it,'' Cade admitted.

''Sure, I can meet them. Do you want me to walk them down this morning?''

Cade shook his head. ''I'll take them down before I ride out.''

Cade and his sons had hearty appetites. Randi realized she could have made more pancakes and they would have eaten those, too. She'd have to remember to increase the recipe next time.

As the boys finished eating, Cade said, ''Tim and Sean, how about if you go collect your dirty clothes and take them to the basement. Gregory, I'd like to talk to you. Let's go to the living room.''

The younger boys scurried upstairs and Gregory followed his father. Randi heard him ask, ''Did I do somethin' wrong?''

''No, there's just something I want to give you,'' Cade responded.

Instead of trying to eavesdrop, knowing the conversation was none of her business, Randi cleared the table and began washing the dishes. Tim and Sean clomped down the stairs to the basement. A short time later, Gregory came to her side and stared up at her. ''Look what Dad gave me.''

Randi took the wallet photo Gregory held out to

her and examined it closely. Cade had his arm curled around a pretty blonde. She posed for the camera while Cade looked down lovingly. A foreign emotion pinched Randi's heart. She'd have to scrutinize the feeling more closely when she didn't have an eight-year-old waiting for her to say something.

"Is this your mom?"

"She's pretty, isn't she?"

Again an unnamed emotion gripped Randi's heart—not only because of Cade and the woman together, but because of the pride in Gregory's voice. "Yes, she is."

"Dad said I can keep it."

Randi handed the picture back to him. "When I go into town today, would you like me to find a picture frame? That will keep it safe."

Gregory nodded. "Yeah. Then it won't get lost." All of a sudden the eight-year-old wrapped his arms around Randi's waist and hugged her. "Thanks, Randi."

She ruffled his hair and murmured, "Anytime, pal." Her throat was too tight to say anything more.

Gregory released her and said, "I'm gonna show Tim and Sean." With that, he scrambled off down to the basement.

Cade came into the kitchen then. "I thought about what you said."

"You didn't burn them all?" She blinked away the moisture that had gathered in her eyes.

"I found that one and a couple of others in the Bible. I have them if Sean and Tim ask." Slowly Cade approached her. With each step he took, her heart beat faster. "It was nice of you to offer to get the frame."

With him standing less than six inches from her, the air in the kitchen rapidly thinned. "Do you need anything else?"

His brown eyes spoke of deeper needs, a man's needs, that had nothing to do with going into town for supplies. "Charlie knows what I want. At least, he always has up till now."

When she took a deep breath, Cade's gaze went to the pulse at her throat, rested on her lips for a moment that seemed like forever, then returned to her eyes. The only sound was the tick...tick...tick of the clock on the wall. Both of them seemed frozen between what they should do and what they would like to do. Randi remembered their kisses, every exciting second of them. But she knew Cade was fighting his desire. She could feel his restraint as much as his need.

And her needs? She hadn't known they existed until she'd met Cade. She'd never imagined they could be so demanding—or so frightening. Cade must have seen the fear as well as the desire, because he reached out and stroked her cheek. "Randi, I..."

The sound of three little boys racing up the stairs and into the kitchen stopped Cade cold. She turned back to the sink to finish the dishes, and she felt him step away.

She shouldn't be feeling so much so fast. But she was, and she would have to deal with it. After Cade and the boys left. After she stopped trembling.

Chapter Five

The fish weren't biting, at least not where Cade dropped his line with Sean and Gregory. He really couldn't spare time off for fishing. But the beautiful, crisp, October Sunday afternoon might be the last such one they saw. Winter was moving in. Cade could smell it in the air, see it in the scrub brush, feel it in his bones. He just prayed the snow would hold off until they moved the cattle to winter pastures at the end of the month.

They'd be getting ready for roundup in the next week or so, and there was still maintenance work to do before winter set in. He'd gotten behind this year. Buck and Al had come down with the flu a few weeks back, one right after the other. Then Cade had spent so much time finding housekeepers. Although

Charlie had watched the boys most days this summer while Cade worked with Al and Buck, his sons were always on his mind. He would check on them every couple of hours, and that took him away from the ranch's demands. He'd gotten more accomplished in the past week—

Because of Randi.

She'd pretty much taken over the house—meals, laundry, cleaning. They'd all fallen into a rhythm practically overnight. But he didn't want to take advantage of her. If she was going to stay on longer, he should offer to pay her. It was only fair.

The sun flirted with the strands of red in her hair as she sat with Tim farther along, up the creek. They'd all been surprised at the practiced way she baited a hook and cast her line. He'd stayed away from her as much as possible this past week. She tempted his self-control too sorely. For the first time in his life, he didn't know if he could rely on the restraint that had always kept him from acting recklessly, that had always insured him from consequences that would complicate his life.

Gregory nudged Cade's arm. "Dad, I'm gettin' hungry."

Sean wiggled on the bank, mumbling, "An' cold."

The temperature had been in the fifties but the sun was sinking. Putting his rod on the bank, Cade shoved himself up and brushed off the seat of his pants. "I'll see if Randi and Tim are ready."

Keeping his eye on Gregory and Sean, Cade made his way toward Randi. She and Tim had chosen a spot about twenty-five yards away. They didn't hear him approach, and he had to smile at the picture they made. Randi blew on her hands and rubbed them together as Tim sat propped with his arm brushing hers.

Cade heard his son's high-pitched voice first.

"I just can't remember 'em," Tim complained. "There's too many."

"You don't have to remember all of the states, do you?"

"No, but some kids remember an awful lot. When Miss Thompson asks, they give her a whole bunch."

"And you want to be able to do that, too."

Tim nodded. "Dad says to always do our best. I wanna do the best."

Cade frowned. Why hadn't Tim told him he was having problems with social studies? A branch snapped under Cade's boot and Randi turned around. When she smiled, his stomach somersaulted.

"So…are we having fish for supper?" she asked.

"Not unless you two caught more than we did."

Tim scrambled to his feet. "Not one. They must be sleepin'."

"More likely, they're just a lot smarter than we think. It looks like we'll have leftovers for supper."

Tim turned up his nose and Randi chucked him playfully on the chin. "We can take that beef I made yesterday and turn it into barbecue. Maybe you and Sean and Gregory can mix up some biscuits to scoop it over."

"Biscuits? Oh, boy. I'm gonna go tell them." Tim ran toward his brothers.

Randi laughed. "They're going to be brimming with energy tonight after sitting so long this afternoon."

For some reason Cade felt defensive. "They like to fish."

She looked up at him speculatively. "I didn't say they didn't."

Cade picked up Tim's pole and reached for hers. "I suppose I should tell you there's talk in Hampton."

She rose to her feet. "About?"

"You. Who you are. What you're doing at the ranch. When the hands were in town last night, they got all kinds of questions."

She stared deep into his eyes. "Am I supposed to be concerned?"

"Maybe, if you value your reputation."

That got her dander up. Her eyes shot silver sparks. "Of course, I value my reputation. What I don't value is giving too much weight to gossip or living my life differently because of it."

"You're not in New York City now," he said in a low voice.

"What's that supposed to mean?"

"It means that in New York there are too many people for each one to care what the other's doing."

"Are you trying to tell me that word's going 'round that you and I are having an affair?"

Cade felt a flush on his cheeks. "That's the gossip."

"And how did Al and Buck and Charlie deal with it?"

"They tried to put people straight. But let's face it—you don't look like any of the housekeepers I had here before."

"So how I *look* defines how I act?" Her voice rose and he could tell she was building up steam.

"I just thought you should know."

"So now I know. And it doesn't make one whit of difference unless—"

"Dad! Dad-deee! Sean fell in the stream!" Gregory yelled.

Cade swore, dropping the poles and taking off toward the boys. He should have known better than to take his eyes off them. He should have known better than to let Randi distract him, with her red hair, deep blue eyes, and simmering passion. Damn! If anything happened to Sean...

Randi reached Sean the same time he did. She'd sprinted out of nowhere. The four-year-old was sitting on the edge of the creek, his jeans soaked and covered with mud, the side of his jacket just as wet and dirty.

Tim said, "We were just foolin' around. I grabbed his pole and he wouldn't let go, then…"

Cade lifted Sean into his arms. "I told you roughhousing along the creek is *not* a good idea. Now, you know. Get your things. Let's go."

Tim's eyes filled with tears. "Dad, I'm sorry.…"

Cade sighed and looked down at his son—the middle one, who'd never gotten as much attention as Gregory or Sean *because* he came between them. "I know you are. But I want to get your brother out of these wet clothes and make sure he's okay. Go on and get your rod and Randi's. I'm going ahead."

Gregory kept up with him. When he glanced over his shoulder, he saw Randi hang her arm around Tim's shoulders. He was glad she was there.

Back at the house, he stripped off Sean's wet and dirty clothes and ran him a hot bath. While Cade took fresh clothes for his son from the dresser drawer, he heard the clatter of dishes in the kitchen.

A few minutes later, Randi appeared at the top of the steps. "Anything I can do to help?"

"He seems fine. Just wet and cold. Could you help him get dressed? I want to talk to Tim."

"Sure, no problem."

As Cade went down the stairs, he didn't think he'd ever met a woman as competent as Randi, a woman who was able to roll with the punches the way she did. *And one who was so damn sexy without half trying.*

When he entered the kitchen, Gregory was dumping flour into a mixing bowl. Tim looked away. "Tim, come into the living room," Cade instructed.

His middle son followed him and sat on the sofa next to him, but still evaded his gaze. "Tim, look at me," Cade commanded gently.

Tim lifted his chin but his lower lip quivered. "I knew you'd be mad."

Cade shook his head. "I'm not mad. I'm worried that someday I won't be within shouting distance if you or Gregory or Sean need me. I understand that what happened today was an accident. But that creek is just as dangerous as an unbroken bronco. You have to be careful when you're around it, and you have to watch out for your brothers, too. Can you do that for me?"

Tim bobbed his head solemnly.

"Good." Cade smiled and opened his arms. "Now give me a hug and we'll forget about it."

Tim hugged him fiercely and as always when Cade felt those small arms around his neck, his heart filled with so much love it ached.

A few minutes later, he left Tim and Gregory carefully pouring milk into the mixing bowl. The boys informed him Randi had measured it for them before she went upstairs. Wondering if she'd found everything she'd needed to dress Sean, Cade returned to the second floor and stopped outside the boys' room.

Randi was kneeling on the floor beside Sean's bed, helping him with his shoes.

Sean said, "I didn't catch no fish."

"Next time," she reassured him as he pushed his foot into the sneaker.

"I don't like fishin'," he said as he peered down at her deft treatment of his shoelaces.

"You don't? I thought it was one of your favorite things to do."

"Uh-uh. I have to sit quiet. I get tired."

She held out the other shoe, and he slipped his foot into it. "You ought to tell your dad."

Sean shook his head vigorously. "He *likes* fishin'."

For the second time today, Cade had learned something new about his sons. And for the second time, he wondered what kind of father he was. Could his sons be afraid of him? Sure, he disciplined them, but he would never raise a hand to them. Each time they misbehaved, he racked his brain to think of a practical punishment—not one that would make them feel bad but one that would teach them. Yet, here they were confiding in a stranger instead of in him!

Did they need a woman's touch so badly? Randi was gentle and compassionate, yet had a sense of humor, too. But she'd be leaving soon. The boys shouldn't get attached. He suddenly realized it was already too late. Still, if she left sooner rather than later...

Maybe they should discuss it. Or maybe after a few more days of playing housekeeper, she'd get tired of it and leave on her own. His stomach clenched. *You're hungry, that's all.*

Since Sean and Randi were unaware of his presence, he left it that way and went back downstairs. He'd help supper along and appease the hunger. Then he'd wait. Randi would tire of ranch life. Soon.

On Wednesday afternoon, Gregory and Tim sat at the table doing their homework while Sean colored. Randi stirred the stew simmering on the stove. She and the boys had fallen into an after-school routine. They liked being in the kitchen while she cooked. It made sense to her because she could help them with homework if they needed it. Homework didn't usually take very long. She was amazed at how much she enjoyed helping Gregory learn his spelling words or going over math combinations with Tim. Sean usually listened and watched, colored, or ran his cars across the kitchen floor.

Randi realized she cared about these three boys very much. Maybe too much. And she was enjoying caring for Sean, going for walks with him and seeing the world from his eyes, taking care of the house, cooking and catching up on reading. Maybe she was enjoying all of it a little *too* much. She told herself it was just a vacation. But then Cade would enter the room and her pulse would race, her heart would pound, their gazes would meet and she'd be aware this was his house, his sons, his life, and she had better be very sure if she wanted more than a vacation.

Something was bothering Cade. But she realized he wasn't about to tell her what it was. After he put the boys to bed each evening, he went to his room. He didn't spend a minute alone with her if he could help it. She could feel the tension building, and she didn't know what to do about it. They hadn't finished the conversation they'd started on Sunday before Sean had fallen into the creek. But with Cade avoiding her if he could, finishing anything wasn't likely.

Randi heard the rattle of a truck approaching the house. Peering out the window, she smiled. It was the parcel service, and she knew exactly what they were delivering. The boys would be surprised and, she hoped, pleased. She stood at the door before the deliveryman knocked. When she opened it, he brought the packages inside and set them on the floor. Then, with a smile and a nod, he was gone.

Gregory jumped from his chair. "What's that?"

Tim scurried around the table and examined the bottom box that stood two feet high.

Sean stared at the flat box on top. "Are they yours?"

Randi laughed. "Nope. They belong to the three of you. But you have to share."

"It's not even Christmas!" Gregory lifted the large flat box and put it on the table. "Can we open them?"

Randi took a pair of scissors from the utensil drawer. "That's the idea." After snipping the tape on one end, she pulled open the flap and slid out a colorful wooden puzzle of the fifty states.

"Look at that."

"Wow!"

"Can I see?"

"What's going on?" Cade asked from the doorway. "I was in the corral when the truck pulled up. Did Charlie order something?"

"No, I did," Randi explained, delighted with the eager curiosity on the boys' faces. "That's a puzzle they can all put together." Using the scissors, she opened the second box and lifted out a globe. "And with this they can learn about traveling to different continents and countries, take out library books that will tell them everything they want to know. Later on, they can figure out miles and longitude and latitude, time changes—" Seeing the tight expression on Cade's face, she stopped.

But the boys didn't. They chattered a mile a minute, spun the globe, and checked out the puzzle pieces. Gregory dumped the puzzle on the table. "Let's put it together!"

Cade captured Randi by the elbow and guided her into the living room. "We need to talk."

There was no point in beating around the bush. "I hope you don't mind that I—"

"I *do* mind. I know what my sons need, and I can take care of what they need."

She didn't understand Cade's anger. "They didn't cost that much."

"Dammit, Randi. I know how much globes cost. But that's not the point. You took it upon yourself to interfere like some benevolent favorite aunt—and you're not!"

His point hurt her more than it should have. "I know I'm not. But Tim's having some trouble—"

"And he should be telling *me* about it, not you."

"So you're acting like a wounded bear because you're jealous? Why does it matter who gets them something they can use?"

"It matters because you have no right to be buying them presents."

For the past week and a half, Randi had put Cade and his sons first. She'd started out doing it to keep her mind on something other than what had happened in New York. But she'd continued doing it because she cared about them...all *four* of them. "I see. So you consider me giving them gifts to be the same as your sons taking candy from a stranger. It's

enlightening to know that's how you think of me.''
She spun around and headed for the kitchen.

"Where are you going?" he demanded.

"Out. I need some fresh air. *You* can make sure
the stew doesn't burn." And with that, she grabbed
her jacket, opened the door, and jogged toward the
stable.

Once inside, she knew exactly what she was going
to do—go for a ride. She'd saddled horses before.
Summer was such a placid animal, Randi knew the
mare wouldn't give her any trouble. In no time at
all, she'd saddled the bay and headed toward the
route Cade had taken the day after she'd arrived.

Randi hadn't gone very far before she realized her
jacket wasn't enough protection against the cold. But
her hurt kept her from turning back. She had to figure out why Cade's rejection hurt so badly. She had
to figure out whether or not she should leave.

The fact was, she wasn't ready to go back. The
fact was, the idea of leaving—

"Randi! Randi, hold up."

She would recognize that voice anywhere. She
hadn't expected him to come after her, and she
wasn't ready to face him again. He hadn't given her
time to figure anything out. She took off at a fast
trot, needing the wind in her face, needing to let her
mind work, needing to let her heart feel.

But Cade wouldn't allow her that luxury.

She felt as if she was in the midst of one of those

old black-and-white Westerns as Cade pulled up beside her and grabbed hold of Summer's reins. "What the hell do you think you're doing?" he asked, his voice deep and angry.

"I was trying to go for a ride." She attempted to yank the reins away from him but he wouldn't let go.

He pulled up closer to her, so close their legs brushed. Every inch of her was cold except for where denim touched denim, where his heat touched hers. He jiggled the reins for emphasis. "Don't you *ever* go riding alone again. Do you hear me?"

She lifted her chin. "I'm not deaf, Cade."

"No, just stupid," he snapped. "The sun's going down, the temperature's dropping, and you're out here playing Annie Oakley. Where are your brains, Randi?"

"I must have left them in New York along with my winter coat and spike heels. If you're going to prevent me from riding, then we might as well go back so I can get warm." This time when she yanked, he let the reins slide through his gloved fingers.

Then he produced a blanket from under his arm and shook it open. "Wrap this around you. And *don't* argue with me."

She was cold enough to do what he said and intuitive enough to realize that if she didn't, he would do it for her. She'd never described a man with the word *macho* before. But Cade fit the bill. At least at the moment.

At the barn, she slipped off the blanket and slid to the ground, then she led Summer inside. With nervous energy borne of the knowledge there was a confrontation to come, she unsaddled Summer and went to the tack room for the grooming brush.

Cade met her there and before she could pick up the brush, he swung her around. "Why did you go running off like that?"

She met his anger with surface courage she'd perfected in the courtroom. "I told you I needed to think."

"About staying or leaving?" he pressed.

"Both. Apparently I'm in the way. If you still think of me as a stranger, then obviously I'm doing things you don't like, especially with the boys—"

The words became a gasp of surprise as Cade took her face between his hands and crushed his lips to hers. She forgot she was upset, she forgot to be cold, she forgot her name. His kiss was the culmination of pent-up restraint and frustration, anger, and desire ready to burst its boundaries. It should have scared her sneakers off, but it didn't. It made her long for more.

Cade broke away, only to surround her with his arms, only to bring his lips to hers again. The scent of hay mingled with the scent of leather, wood, and Cade himself. Tight against him, she tried to tell herself she didn't have to fall in deeper. But his hard body against her softer one evoked feelings that burned and ached to be set free. And not only feelings, but needs—needs that could put her heart in danger because they were as potent as the lure of paradise. Cade could take her there; she both knew it and feared it.

Where was her logic? Where was her caution? Where was her control? All of them fled with the pressing aggression of Cade's lips, the taunting invasion of his tongue. She kept telling herself she could keep her feet on the ground, but when Cade's tongue stroked hers, the universe swayed and she felt the earth tremble. He kissed her as if she were the only woman in the world—the only woman in the world for him.

Cade fought the anger and the need and the desire. But they were as demanding as fire gone wild over dry brush. The anger came at him from more than one place—anger at himself for giving in to a need, for putting that hurt in Randi's eyes, for not being enough of a father to his sons. The need had stung before, but never this deeply, never with this gut-wrenching fist hold. And the desire—it whipped him until he had to give in to it.

He wasn't sorry about giving in. Not yet. Not while he was tasting Miranda and holding her and relishing the passion that was bringing his body to life with each stroke of his tongue, each breath that took in her scent, each press against her that was a bit of heaven and a bit of hell at the same time. His hunger for her seemed outrageously out of proportion, alarming and puzzling. If he could just satisfy some of it...

The kiss turned wilder and the hunger increased instead of diminished. He pressed her tight against him, hating the barriers of his coat, her jacket. When he rocked his hips against hers, she arched toward him, meeting his need, inflaming his arousal, making him want so much he hurt.

The hurt wouldn't quit with a roll in the hay or a meeting between the sheets. It was still too raw for sex to satisfy. It was too raw to ever heal. He wasn't about to use Randi as a bandage. And that was all she would ever be. Because she would leave, just like Susan.

With a groan from deep in his soul, he lifted his head and pulled away.

Randi frowned, her forehead creased, the passionate glaze left her eyes. They were fathomless blue and confused. He didn't feel so sure of anything himself.

"Do you want to forget that one, too?" she asked with an edge of accusation.

"Not possible," he muttered, trying to put everything in perspective.

"At least we agree on that."

He took a deep breath, then in a rush said, "I'm

grateful for everything you've done since you've been here. And I'm not jealous.''

''What, then?'' Her determined tone said she wouldn't let it go.

He wasn't used to putting private thoughts into words. ''I have to wonder what kind of father I am. Gregory talks to you about Susan. Tim confides he's having problems with social studies. Sean's afraid to tell me he doesn't like to go fishing. Why can't they talk to me? Why didn't they come to me?''

The confusion vanished from Randi's eyes and the compassion he was coming to know as part of her took its place. ''Cade, you're a fine father. The problem, if there is one, is that you do everything right.''

He'd never expected Randi to engage in idle flattery. He plucked the grooming brush from the shelf. ''I'm not a fool, Randi, so don't play me for one.''

As he strode toward the stalls, she grabbed his arm. ''Listen to me, Cade. Your sons idolize you. They think you're perfect. Maybe even all-knowing. They think you can do no wrong, let alone make a mistake. And that's terrific because you make a great role model. But it also presents a problem. They don't want to let you down. They might pull pranks to run off housekeepers they don't like, but basically they want your approval.''

He saw the sincerity on her face and felt the caring in her touch. ''You're serious.''

She released his arm and as if she was afraid the

fire between them would burst into flame spontane-
ously, she took a step back. "Let me tell you about
approval, Cade. Because I wanted my father's approval, I stretched all my abilities to their limits
whether it was playing girls' basketball or bringing
home a boy he'd approve of. Trying so hard made
me a perfectionist and that's come in handy. But it
took me all these years to learn I can't be the best
for someone else, because it might never be good
enough. I have to be the best for myself. And if I'm
not the best or right or I make a mistake, I have to
live with that, too."

"And the point is?"

"Show them you're human, Cade. Admit when
you're wrong. Tell them you make mistakes, too,
and let them love you when you do. Then they'll
see *they're* okay whether they fail or succeed. And
they'll know you'll love *them* either way."

This woman flabbergasted him sometimes. Here
he thought he had to do everything right, and she
was telling him to show-and-tell his sons when he
screwed up. Could she be right? "Maybe they just
need a woman to talk to. And if that's the case, I'm
glad it's you they're talking to."

Randi looked surprised. Her eyes got big and soft
and all he wanted to do was experience the wild
passion between them again. But he knew better.
"We need to talk about a financial arrangement."

The softness left her eyes to be replaced by wariness. "What kind of arrangement?"

"I want to pay you. You're doing a lot more than earning room and board." He named a sum he thought was fair.

"I don't need your money."

"Whether you do or not doesn't matter. I need to pay you so I'm not worrying about repaying you. I don't want to owe you. I don't like to owe anybody."

She studied him long enough to make him feel uncomfortable. Finally, she agreed, "If you insist." It was obvious she wasn't happy about it.

"There's something else I insist on, too. *Don't* go riding alone. I mean it, Randi. If you do it again, I'll send you packing. Too much can happen."

Instead of fighting him, like he thought she might, she nodded. "I wasn't thinking. I just needed breathing space."

Her lips were so pink and sweet, her skin so delectably touchable. It was damn hard for him to keep his hands by his sides. "Believe me, I understand." Maybe now, the tension between them wouldn't be so taut. Maybe now, they'd worked the desire out of their systems.

"Is Charlie with the boys?" she asked.

Cade nodded. "He saw you riding out and came to get me."

Randi picked up a brush from the shelf.

He took it from her. "I'll take care of the horses. I'm sure the boys would like your help with that puzzle."

She passed by him, her shoulder grazing his. "I won't get them anything else unless I talk to you about it first."

"Randi?"

She stood still.

"Thanks for caring about my boys."

She smiled. "It's easy to care about them, Cade."

When he didn't respond, she crossed to the door.

As he watched her leave the barn, he knew he was only fooling himself if he thought their passion was spent. If anything, that kiss had only whetted his appetite for more.

He told himself again, *She won't be staying.*

The devil on his shoulder asked, *And what if she does?*

He didn't have the answers, and he wished to high heaven he did.

Chapter Six

Two weeks later, Randi closed the book she'd been reading. The boys were upstairs changing into their pajamas. Cade had gone to the barn to check on a horse that had gone lame.

Cade.

Sometimes he looked at her as if kissing her was the foremost thing on his mind. The heat in his gaze often made her look away. Yet he kept distance between them—physical and emotional. Since their kiss in the barn, she'd realized she was falling in love with him. And not only with *him*, but with his sons. Day by day, they were taking over more of her heart.

She'd watched Cade during roundup. She'd seen the fatigue but satisfaction on his face after the calves had been weaned and shipped. She'd witnessed how neighbors worked together to help each other. This was a challenging dream Cade had chosen, but a fulfilling one.

Surprisingly, she felt fulfilled, too. And free. Of someone else's expectations. She had never felt more free. Or more confused. Just because she was falling in love with Cade didn't mean he was falling in love with her. In fact—

The phone rang and she jumped. Putting her book on the coffee table, she picked up the receiver.

"Hello. Gallagher residence."

"I'd...I'd like to talk to Miranda Sinclair," a hesitant female voice said.

"I'm Miranda Sinclair. How can I help you?" Randi didn't recognize the voice.

"You don't know me. I'm a neighbor of Cade's." Randi waited for the rest of the explanation.

"I...uh...I hear you're a lawyer."

"Yes, I am."

"I wondered if I could talk to you."

"Are you in trouble?"

"It's a marriage matter. I don't have much money. Just some extra I saved from groceries. That's why I can't go to the lawyer in town. I thought maybe because I knew Cade..." Her tone was forlorn but slightly hopeful.

"What's your name?" Randi asked gently.

"Laura Thorn."

"Laura, I can't practice law in Montana."

"I know you're from New York, but I thought maybe you could just give me some advice."

"Would you like to come over?"

"No. I mean, I don't want Ned, my husband, to know. Could I meet you at the One Horse Café in Hampton? Anybody seeing two women talking wouldn't suspect I'm getting advice from you. They'd probably think Cade introduced us and we're gettin' to know each other."

Laura had apparently thought this through very carefully. "I'd like to run a few errands in Hampton. Would Friday be good for you?"

"Friday's fine. I can get my mom to watch the twins. You don't know how much I appreciate this. Is ten o'clock all right?"

"Ten is fine."

"Miss Sinclair? Please don't say anything about this to anyone."

"I won't."

When Randi hung up, she wondered if she was doing the right thing. She didn't want to keep anything from Cade. It was the first time since she'd been practicing law that she'd ever thought twice about lawyer-client confidentiality. But it wasn't negotiable. It just was.

"Randi! Randi!" Gregory called from the top of the steps. "Can you come up? Sean doesn't feel good."

Usually Cade put the boys to bed. It was a special time he enjoyed with his sons and Randi didn't want to horn in if she wasn't wanted. In the time since she'd been here, he'd never asked her to help.

The four-year-old had been quiet today, not wanting to take a walk or even visit the horses in the barn. At supper, she'd noticed he'd eaten less than usual. She took the steps two at a time, not knowing what to expect upstairs.

Tim and Gregory stood in the bathroom, and little Sean was sitting on the side of the bathtub. They were dressed in assorted colors of plaid pajamas. Sean's were red and white. His top was unbuttoned.

Tim said, "He felt like he was gonna…you know." He wrinkled his nose.

She lifted Sean into her arms and tilted her forehead against his. "So you're not feeling so well."

He shook his head and looked ready to cry. "It's my tummy."

He felt warm to the touch but not burning hot. "Let's get you into your bed and under the covers."

Gregory's forehead creased. "But what if he has to—"

"Does your dad have a basin?" Randi asked as she carried Sean to his room.

"We can look in the basement," Tim offered.

"That's a good idea. I want to talk to Sean a little."

"Is he gonna be okay?" Tim asked with a worried frown.

Randi said, "I think so. It's probably just a virus." While Tim and Gregory went downstairs, she sat on Sean's bed with him on her lap. "Do you mind if I feel your tummy to see if it hurts?"

The little boy's eyes were wide and trusting. He shook his head.

When Cade returned to the house, Randi wasn't anywhere downstairs. He climbed the steps, hearing the boys chattering in their room. He reached the doorway and stopped short.

Randi was propped up in Sean's bed, with Sean on her lap and an afghan from the foot covering them both. Tim and Gregory sat cross-legged at her feet. Sean's head lay nestled in the crook of her shoulder. Cade's chest tightened as he tried to absorb the scene—a scene from that dream he'd once had.

"What's going on?" he asked, not quite able to keep the huskiness from his voice.

"Sean's sick," Gregory explained.

Cade noticed the bucket by the side of the bed and crossed to his son. "What's the matter, partner?"

"Randi says I have a virus."

Cade's gaze found hers and he had to swallow hard. Her ponytail lay over her shoulder. Her hair drifted down her breast. Her pink sweater was the same color as the soft flush on her cheeks as she held Sean close to her. She looked like a mother.

"Do you have a thermometer? I'd like to take his temperature," Randi said, interrupting his train of thought. "I bet it's about ninety-nine, but we should make sure. His stomach's upset but he doesn't have any tender spots." She gently rubbed her chin against Sean's forehead. It was an unconscious gesture of caring—Cade could tell.

"I have one in my dresser. Be right back."

Cade urged Gregory and Tim to crawl into their bunk beds while they waited for the plastic-covered children's thermometer to register. When Cade removed it from Sean's mouth, it was ninety-nine on the dot. He brushed Sean's hair away from his forehead. "Do you think you can fall asleep?"

Sean shook his head and nestled deeper into Randi's shoulder. "Can Randi read me a story?"

Cade lifted his sleeve and checked his watch. It was already past the boys' bedtime. "Tim and Gregory have to get to sleep or they'll be dragging in school tomorrow. You and Randi can move to my room. I'll go get some soda to settle your stomach. Okay?"

"Can she read to us tomorrow night?" Tim asked from his bed.

"That's up to her." Cade didn't know if it would be good to start a routine with his sons that wouldn't last.

"Sure, I can," Randi agreed.

Cade went over to his sons, pulled their covers up to their chins, and ruffled their hair. "I'll see you in the morning." Then he scooped Sean from Randi's lap and carried the little boy to the master bedroom.

He heard Randi's soft good-nights and Tim and Gregory's answering responses. When he flicked on the light in his bedroom, he wondered why her gentle mothering made him hurt so. He turned back the bedclothes and set Sean on the bed.

Randi came in, a book in her hand, and hesitated. "Maybe you'd like your dad to read to you."

Sean shook his head. "I want you."

"Go ahead," Cade commanded gruffly. "I'll go get the soda."

He tried not to think or feel as he mechanically popped open a can and poured the beverage into a small glass. He kept seeing Randi rubbing her chin against Sean's forehead. And it made him ache.

When he returned to the bedroom, he set the glass on the nightstand, then sat in the bedroom chair, propping his feet on the bed. He'd wait until Sean fell asleep, then carry him back to his room.

Randi did a good job reading the book. She didn't even sound as if she was reading. And Sean's eyes didn't droop as they usually did. When she closed the book, the four-year-old asked, "Can you *tell* me a story? Not one I heard before?"

Randi chuckled and looked at Cade.

He shrugged. "I'm not good at making them up."

"I can try. My brothers and I used to spin some good ones."

Cade listened as Randi started out with a cowboy and took him on an adventure across the Montana range. By the time she wrapped it up, Sean's eyes had almost closed.

Cade pulled his boots from the edge of the bed to the floor. Then he stepped close to the bed to lift Sean into his arms. When he stooped down, he smelled the scent Randi used. He didn't know if it was shampoo, lotion or perfume, but whatever it was it urged him to close his eyes, breathe deeply and envision his bed with her and him in it—naked. And when his hand brushed her breast as he slid it under his son, he heard her catch of breath and feared he was fighting a losing battle. He was aroused and he couldn't do a damn thing about it.

To make matters worse, Sean suddenly opened his eyes and gripped Randi around the neck. "I want to stay here and sleep."

Randi tried to help. "Your dad can crawl in with you."

"I want *you*," Sean argued, curling tighter against her.

Cade gave a resigned sigh. Randi was softness and gentleness that was hard to resist. So how could he blame his son for wanting to stay exactly where he was!

Randi lifted her gaze to Cade's. "I don't mind sleeping here with him."

He looked down over her sweater and jeans and said brusquely, "Tell me where your nightgown is and I'll get it."

Her cheeks flared a delicious pink and he wondered if her thoughts were as X-rated as his. But her voice didn't give anything away when she answered, "Inside the closet door on the hook."

It wasn't until Cade held the nightgown in his hand, ran his fingers over the white cotton and inhaled her scent, that he decided having this particular woman sharing his house was becoming pure torture. But what could he do? The boys needed her.

The next morning Cade opened the door to his own room feeling like an intruder. His back felt like hell after trying to sleep on the sofa, but he hadn't even contemplated sleeping in Randi's bed. Just the thought of her, let alone her scent on the sheets, would have driven him crazy. He needed a change of clothes or he wouldn't be going anywhere near her now.

When he stepped into his room, he first looked at Sean, then stepped closer and felt his forehead. He didn't feel particularly warm. Sprawled on his stomach, one hand dangling over the edge of the bed, Sean looked as comfortable as he always did when he slept.

Try as he might, Cade couldn't keep his gaze away from Randi. She lay on her side, turned toward Sean, her hair fanned out on the white pillowcase. Cade took a deep breath as he studied the sleep-relaxed contours of her face. She was a beautiful woman. Unfortunately, he couldn't resist looking at more than her face. Her nightgown had slipped side-ways, revealing one creamy shoulder. The covers had slipped to her waist, and he could see her breast outlined by the cotton. Every muscle in his body tightened. Some throbbed, and he almost groaned.

Whether he did groan and didn't realize it, or whether he shifted and a board creaked, or whether his sudden desire connected with something in Randi that was even more powerful than a sixth sense, she opened her eyes and stared right at him. He felt like a kid with his hand caught in the cookie jar.

Heat crept up his neck, but he stood his ground. "Go back to sleep. I have to get some clothes." His voice was a hoarse rumble that even he didn't rec-ognize.

Her blue eyes started at his face, but swept down his open shirt and lingered on the mat of hair on his chest. Whatever the pull was between them, it had never been stronger. In fact, if Sean hadn't been sleeping in that bed…

Cade turned away, opened the closet door, and took a shirt silently from a hanger. Then he closed the door and said, "Don't get up. I'll get the boys off to school. I'll check with you at lunch to see how Sean's doing.''

With that, Cade left the room and closed the door. As he did, he realized he'd forgotten socks and underwear. He wasn't going back in. Not for all the cattle in the state of Montana. Some things just weren't worth the risk.

Charlie brought the all-purpose vehicle to the front of the house Friday morning, hopped out, and handed Randi the keys. ''Don't worry about being back for lunch. I'll take care of Sean.''

She took the keys from him. ''I should be back. But there's still chicken soup in the refrigerator.''

Charlie smiled. ''And what about a cookie if he asks for it?''

''Give him half a cookie. If he feels okay tonight he can have the other half.'' She'd kept Sean on a crackers-and-toast diet until last night when he'd had soup and felt fine.

The old cowhand's expression suddenly became serious. ''You're doin' a fine job with those boys. A right fine job. It's a shame you're a high-priced lawyer or you might think about staying.''

Staying. With Cade and his sons. She didn't miss New York one little bit.

''Would you?'' Charlie prodded.

''What?''

''Think about staying.''

Before she thought better of it, she responded, "That would depend on Cade." Then she looked Charlie straight in the eye. "That's between you and me, Charlie."

His eyes twinkled and he smiled. "If you say so. I haven't gotten to be this old without knowin' when to keep my mouth shut. But, you know, Miss Randi, maybe that's somethin' Cade ought to know you're considerin'."

She shook her head. "That's the problem, Charlie. I don't even know if I should be."

He shrugged. "There's only one lawyer in Hampton now and he's got a monopoly. A little competition would do him good." With that, Charlie stepped away from the vehicle so she could climb in.

After she did, she waited to close the door. "I'll think about what you said. And thanks, Charlie, for watching Sean for me. I'll be back by one at the latest."

The cowhand tipped his hat, and she closed the door.

The small town of Hampton was big as small towns went. Three stoplights controlled traffic on Pine Street. A school, library and three churches, a grocery store and approximately fifteen family-owned businesses—from a bakery and medical center to a saddle shop and a full-service gas station—

lined the stretch through the center of town. The houses on the side streets were mostly older homes. North of the last traffic light, Randi could see an area of houses that looked newer, built with siding rather than clapboard. The lumberyard and the feed mill employed many of the residents who lived in those homes, Charlie had informed Randi on the first trip to town.

When she reached Hampton this time, she drove straight to the One Horse Café and parked along the street, then locked the car and went inside.

The waitresses were serving breakfast as Randi made her way down the aisle between red vinyl booths in the café. She stopped when she came to a young blond-haired woman who nervously turned her coffee cup on its saucer. Not seeing anyone else in the restaurant who would fit the description of a young mother with a lot on her mind, Randi asked, "Laura?"

The blonde smiled shyly. "Miss Sinclair?"

Randi slipped into the seat across from her and nodded. A waitress asked if she wanted coffee and she nodded again.

After the waitress poured another cup, Laura took out a red change purse that had her keys attached. She opened it and took out a wad of bills, offering them to Randi. "It's all I've got. About seventy-five dollars. I know it's not much...."

Randi put her hand over Laura's. "Put your money away. Let's talk."

Laura's eyes opened wide in surprise. "Rod Clemens wanted $150 up front, just to step into his office."

"He's a lawyer?"

"The only one in town."

"I don't know if I can help you. Tell me what the problem is."

"I think I want a divorce." Laura said it in a hushed tone as if she were afraid of the word.

Randi looked Laura over closely. She didn't look a day over twenty. "How old are you, Laura?"

"Twenty-one."

"How long have you been married?"

"Two years."

"You said you have twins. How old are they?"

"Six months." Laura swept her blond bangs from her forehead. "Everything changed when I got pregnant. And now, everything's...awful." Her gray eyes filled with tears.

"Does your husband hurt you?" Randi needed to know exactly what she was dealing with.

"Hurt me?" Laura looked confused for a moment, then shocked. "Oh, no! Ned would *never* do anything like that."

"Why do you want a divorce?"

"Because...because it's like we're not even married anymore. I take care of the twins, I cook, I take care of the twins, I clean, I take care of the twins, and *he's* never around. When we first got married, we lived with my parents till we got our own place built. Ned works the ranch with my dad. And, for a while there, we didn't have any privacy. But we came into town Saturday nights, we snuck off to the unfinished house, we went riding...."

"So you live on your parents' ranch?"

Laura bobbed her head. "I don't know what I'd do without Mom. When the twins won't stop crying or when I've been up a few nights in a row, she spells me. And I know Ned has to work, but he's their father. He should be helping me. I never see him except to feed him and clean up after him."

"Laura, have you talked to your husband about all this?"

"Talk? Who has time to talk? The babies cry, the stock needs to be fed, there always seems to be some emergency...."

Randi took a sip of her coffee. "You called me for advice. It might not seem to be worth the money you wanted to give me, but here it is. Talk to your husband about all this. Tell him what's bothering you."

Laura bit her lower lip. "I don't know how."

"Do you love him, Laura?"

The young woman nodded, her eyes filling with tears again.

"Talk to him," Randi repeated. "Tell him how

you feel and then if you hit a wall, call me again. All right?''

"It might take me a while to work up my nerve," Laura said tentatively.

"You do it when you're ready. But nothing can change until you talk to your husband about what's troubling you."

"He might think I'm just complainin' about things we can't change. He might not want to help. Then what do I do?"

"Then you'll know. Then you can think about what to do next. But you have to start somewhere."

Laura glanced down at her wallet. "Are you sure I don't owe you anything?"

Randi smiled. "I haven't done anything. But you could tell me the best place in town to buy a winter coat."

"Winston's has some nice parkas. Go down to the second light and turn left. It's right there."

The waitress came up then and gave Randi a thorough once-over. "Would you like to see a breakfast menu?"

Randi stood and pulled a dollar bill from her purse, laying it next to her cup. "No, thanks. I have to get going. But that was a great cup of coffee." With a last glance at Laura, she said, "Call me if you need me."

As Randi left the coffee shop, she realized how much she liked feeling needed. She'd felt needed when she'd taken care of her brothers. She'd felt needed when she'd worked for legal aid. In the firm where she worked now, she didn't feel needed as much as used. Her firm's name, her reputation and skill made a difference in courtroom manipulations, but she wasn't sure how much of a difference they made in people's lives.

But here in Montana, she felt different. She felt she was making a difference in Sean, Tim and Gregory's lives—daily. And she felt as if she might have just now made a difference that counted in Laura's.

Had she made a difference in Cade's life?

She might never know the answer.

A week later, on Saturday afternoon as the boys did their chores in the barn under Charlie's supervision, Randi folded laundry on the kitchen table. The wind blew against the kitchen windows, and Randi rubbed her arms over her blue velour tunic top. She could use another layer. The gray sky looked threatening. She knew Cade hoped winter would hold off just a few days longer. He'd moved half the cows to winter pastures and was planning to move the rest starting Monday.

Suddenly the door flew open and Cade came in with about as much force as the wind, his expression as stormy as the sky. "I just had a visitor."

She hadn't heard any cars or trucks.

Cade shrugged off his jacket and stripped off his

gloves. "What makes you think you have the right to go stirring around in my neighbor's business?"

In his flannel work shirt, jeans and boots, Cade looked like a lumberjack. His eyes were troubled, and he stood in a defensive stance that said she had better have some answers. "What makes you think I stirred around in your neighbor's business?" she asked calmly.

"Ned Thorn just rode over. It seems you've been talking to Laura. He said you advised her to get a divorce."

"I did no such thing!"

Cade crossed to her, towering over her. "Then why would he say it?"

"Laura talked to me about *getting* a divorce, but…"

Cade took her by the shoulders. "I've known Ned since I used to come out here for summers and stay with my uncle. He's a good man. He's loved Laura since she was in pigtails and he couldn't do anything about it because she was five years younger than him. But he's always worked for her dad. He's worked damn hard and has a stake in the ranch's future. Why would you even think about messing with these people's lives?"

Cade was talking about Ned and Laura but she sensed his anger and deep concern was more personal than worry about his neighbor's marriage. "Laura called me. She didn't have enough money to pay the lawyer in town, and she heard I was a lawyer. She thought—''

The phone rang.

Cade let go of Randi and snatched it up. After a few short sentences, he handed the phone to her. ''It's Laura.''

Cade's accusing brown eyes didn't leave her as she listened to his neighbor who was crying and talking so fast, Randi could hardly understand her. But she managed to learn that Laura had finally worked up the nerve to talk to Ned but they'd gotten into a monumental argument. He'd stormed out. Finally, when Laura ran down, Randi said, ''I'll meet you in town next week. Let me know when the best time is for you.''

After Randi hung up, Cade's expression was thunderous. ''I can't believe after what I just told you, you're going to help her take the easy way out, shaft Ned—''

Randi pointed her finger at his chest.

''Just you wait a minute, Cade Gallagher. First of all, you apparently don't know Laura's side. And I'm not about to fill you in. I can't if I'm her legal adviser. But don't you believe it's ever as simple as one day you have a marriage and the next day you don't.''

''It happened to me!'' he revealed in a growl that ran through her because it was so raw.

She could feel the bitterness vibrating around him,

but even more than that, she could feel the pain. Stepping closer to him, wanting to wrap her arms around him, she murmured, "Tell me about it."

He swung around, braced his arms on the counter, and stared out the window.

Randi held her breath, knowing that if he told her, if he let the pain out, he would have room for love. Why did she care so much? Her own life was in chaos. It wasn't as if—

You want to stay?

You want Cade to love you?

He spoke then. "We had a life. We had dreams. I thought we shared them."

"What were your dreams, Cade?" she asked quietly.

He turned his head first, as if the sound of her voice was making him slowly face the past. Then he faced her. "My parents have a good marriage. They live for each other—they always have. They have the same values and vision of life. I thought that's what Susan and I would have."

"What went wrong?"

He rubbed his hand across his jaw. "I didn't know her well enough, I guess. I never realized what we wanted was so different. Or maybe I only saw what *I* wanted to see."

Randi kept quiet, knowing Cade had probably gone over all of this a million times in his mind.

"I only landed in New York City to make money

so I could eventually buy into this place. Susan wasn't from the city, either. I took that as a good sign, thinking she'd want to return to a less hectic life. I was wrong. When we moved out here, she expected to have all the conveniences of New York. Even if that was possible, I didn't have the spare cash to oblige—not on an ongoing basis. Ranching is uncertain. It takes investing and reinvesting, and even then…" He threw up his hands. "She didn't understand. She wanted everything right away."

"But the boys. I don't understand how she could leave her sons!" Randi admitted, hurting for three lovable little boys.

"I'm easy to leave, but they wouldn't be?" he asked in the guise of a joke, but the hurt was there.

"Cade…"

The lines on his face cut deep as he shook his head. "I don't want your pity."

She couldn't help reaching out and stroking his jaw. "I don't pity you." Her heart hammered as she realized how much she loved him. But she kept that knowledge to herself. "I'm sorry you and your boys were hurt. I'm sorry Susan couldn't appreciate something deeper and finer than money and conveniences."

He slid his hand under her hair. His fingers were caressing and oh, so seductive. As seductive as his low voice when he said, "You haven't spent a winter here. It's no picnic, Miranda."

She didn't know if he used her full name to distance himself or to remind himself that she came
from New York City and another world. "I could
spend the winter here."

His eyebrows arched and he frowned. "What
about your law practice?"

"I told the firm I'm on a leave of absence till
further notice."

"And they accepted that?"

"They consider me an asset."

He gently tugged on her hair, pulling her head
back. Right before his lips met hers, he murmured,
"So do I."

Cade smelled like the outdoors, and leather, and
all man. She wished she could tell him she loved
him. But she knew Cade didn't trust her yet, and he
needed more than words. Maybe he would never
trust. Maybe he could never again believe in a
woman's love. But she had to take the chance. She
wanted to stay and give him the time he needed to
learn to trust her.

His flannel shirt was soft; his muscles were taut.
When he caressed her back with his large hands, she
opened her lips and invited him to explore and to
trust, to take and to give. Impulse gave way to
heated desire. Cade angled her head and slid his
hands to her waist.

Then abruptly he pushed away and muttered,
"This is going to be a long winter."

They were both breathing hard. The light of passion still blazed in his eyes, and she knew all she'd have to do was touch him and they'd start all over again. But how would they finish?

"Do you want me to stay, Cade?"

His face showed no emotion; his voice was neutral. "The boys need you."

But what about you? her heart asked. She knew he wouldn't answer if she asked; she knew he wouldn't admit he needed anyone. "Then you've got me for the winter."

"Let's just take it day by day," he advised. "No promises. It's better for everyone that way."

He didn't trust her to stay even for the boys. Couldn't he see she would do anything for them? For him? Before she could put her feelings into words, the kitchen door opened and three boys tumbled in.

But Cade didn't step away from her. Instead, he asked, "How would you like to go in to Hampton tonight? There's a band at the Round-Up. Country— not what you're used to..."

"I've always wanted to learn the two-step."

Cade's smile was crooked and altogether endearing. "Then I'll ask Charlie if he'll watch the boys."

Randi said to Cade's sons, "If you wash up and get your hands *really* clean, I might let you help me roll the meatballs."

All three boys broke into smiles as they rushed off to the bathroom.

Cade picked up his jacket and slipped it on. Returning to the reason he'd come inside in the first place, he said, "Randi, I'd like you to stay out of Ned and Laura's marriage."

"If Laura wants me to help her, I don't know if I can stay out of it," she responded as honestly as she could.

Gregory ran back into the kitchen and showed Randi his hands. "I'm ready."

Cade opened the door. "We'll talk more about this later."

Randi had hoped they would get closer tonight. She'd hoped they could simply have a good time. But she was afraid Cade wouldn't let the subject of Ned and Laura drop. And she was sure she'd have to stand her ground. She didn't know how Cade would handle that.

Tonight, she would find out.

Chapter Seven

The subject of Laura and Ned Thorn didn't come up as Cade drove to Hampton. Randi suspected he knew she wouldn't back down, and he didn't want to start the evening with an argument any more than she did. The problem was, even without an argument, the tingling tension connecting them whenever they came within two feet of each other vibrated in the silent darkness.

"It seems funny to be coming into town on a Saturday night," Cade said as they stopped at the traffic light.

"You don't come in with your men?"

"I did a few times after Susan left, when Charlie insisted I get away from the ranch. But Saturday nights I usually catch up on bookwork."

"You don't date?"

He glanced at her in the shadows. "I haven't had the time or the inclination. It's usually more trouble than it's worth."

That comment effectively closed the subject as the light turned green and Cade pushed down on the accelerator.

Half a block later he slowed, then turned into a parking lot. Only a few spaces were vacant. "Full house tonight. I hope you don't mind a crowd."

She laughed. "I'm used to New York City, remember?"

Unlatching his seat belt, he shifted toward her. "I should. But sometimes I forget."

A blast of wind swept against the vehicle.

"Winter's moving in. By later tonight you might wish you were back there."

Before she could frame a response, he'd pushed open his door and come around to hers.

Cold air blasted her as she opened the car door. Cade pulled the brim of his hat low on his brow and offered his hand to help her out. She couldn't remember the last time a man had done something so chivalrous. Cade was an intriguing mixture of polished Easterner and rugged cowboy. She had never met a man as fascinating, as sensual...as distant. Yet there were those brief moments of vulnerability when his sons' welfare was at stake and the fiery

passion that spoke of a hunger for intimacy told her
he yearned for more than distance.

Once she stood beside him, the wind tossed her
hair around her face. Cade gazed down at her, his
height and breadth a staunch protection against the
cold front blowing in. Reaching toward her, he
brushed her hair from her cheek and lifted the hood
of her parka. ''You ought to get a hat, too, and de-
cent gloves. Winter here is bitter, Randi.''

She couldn't even feel the cold—not with Cade
looking at her as if he wanted to kiss her, not with
his hand so close to her cheek. ''The next time I
come to town I'll find the warmest hat and gloves I
can.''

His smile was wry. He closed the car door and
guided her toward the club with his hand on the
small of her back. She liked the feel of his protective
care.

Inside the door Cade took her parka and his suede
coat and checked them. Several people waved and
nodded at Cade as he guided Randi to an empty table
for two. She glanced around, taking in the rough-
hewn beams, the polished wooden bar with the high
stools, the tables for two and four. Some of the men
still wore their Stetsons. Cade had checked his.

Tonight, he wore a chambray shirt with full
sleeves and pearl snap buttons. His black string tie
lay straight on his shirt placket. Black jeans and
boots emphasized the long length of his legs. She

looked at him and she felt so much that she'd never felt before.

At the small table, Cade's gaze drifted over her teal silk blouse and black serge slacks. "I bet it feels good to get off the ranch."

The expression on his face was serious. As the band started playing, she leaned closer to him and her shoulder brushed his. "I don't look at the ranch as a prison, Cade."

"It can be when winter sets in or when work mounts up. Like during calving."

"Tell me about it."

He tilted his head, studying her speculatively, then moved even closer so she would be sure to hear him. "We calve over five hundred cows in about six weeks. So much can go wrong—from birthing improperly to weather extremes. We have to watch the cows almost constantly and we do it in shifts both day and night."

"Why do you do it?" she asked, to discover another reason why he'd chosen ranching.

"Because I love seeing the newborns, living in the cycle of life, meeting the challenge of making each new year a success. I love watching my sons taking it all in, joining in the making of it, learning that a man reaps what he sows."

"And why don't you believe a woman can share in the joy and the work and the learning?" Her face was so close to his. She could see the shadow of his beard even though he'd just shaved. The scent of his soap and a hint of after-shave pleased her sense of smell, while listening to him, appreciating the strong line of his jaw and the deep brown of his eyes, assuaged her other senses. The only sense feeling a loss was touch. She longed to touch him.

Cade thought before he spoke. "Most women aren't hardy enough or giving enough or imaginative enough to see this life as worthwhile. Most women see it as simply hard. Much too hard."

"You're talking about Susan."

He shook his head. "Even women raised here find it hard."

"Cade, any life can be hard. Snow and lots of land, and animals to care for aren't any different than daily traffic jams, crime, and a job that demands every ounce of energy, leaving nothing left over to give joy."

He propped his elbow on the table and gently held her chin in his palm. "Had you lost your joy?"

She couldn't think clearly when he was touching her but she knew her answer could be important to whatever happened between them from this moment on. "Yes, I had. But I found it again taking care of your sons, taking long walks along fields of winter wheat. I feel it most of all when you kiss me."

He dropped his hand and leaned away. "Don't mistake change for joy. And don't mistake desire for anything else than the pleasure it brings."

A hard attitude. But Cade wasn't a hard man. She'd gotten too many glimpses of the tenderness and gentleness in him to believe that he was as tough as his words, or this land, or the barricade he'd created around his heart.

Two lines of dancers formed on the dance floor. Cade pushed back his chair, stood, and smiled down at her. "Let's get you started on something easy."

"Easy?" She glanced over at the dancers, who looked as if they knew exactly what they were doing.

"There's nothing to this one if you've got a little bit of rhythm, and I'm sure you do." He took her hand and tugged her up.

"But I thought you didn't come here. How do you know it's easy?"

He curved his arm around her waist and guided her to one of the lines. "You can't come in here without someone dragging you to the dance floor. Besides, I watch the country channel when I can't sleep." At her skeptical look, he grinned. "I do."

As a dancer in front of the line demonstrated the steps and urged everyone else to try them, Randi noticed Cade didn't miss a beat. When the woman went through it again, he said to Randi, "Left heel out, feet together, right heel out, together, now two right toes, forward, back, forward, back. Got it?"

"You've got to be kidding."

He chuckled. "It's easier with the music. Just relax. Nobody cares if you mess it up."

And she did mess it up, time after time. Until finally halfway through the song, her feet and body connected with the pattern. Soon she realized she was synchronized with Cade. She looked over at him and caught him watching her. His gaze lingered on her silk shirt molding to her breasts. Any banter she might have considered flew out of her head.

When the song ended, he asked her, "Are you game for another one?"

She tried to ignore the heat emanating from both of them as well as Cade's appeal, while everything about him—from the lock of hair falling across his brow to the toes of his black boots—pulled her toward him. "Sure, I'm game. Just don't be surprised if my feet land on yours."

"I'll risk it," he said, his voice deep and husky.

The second dance was more complicated than the first. Randi had to give it every ounce of her concentration so she didn't end up in the line in front of her or fall behind everyone else. When she moved sideways, she tripped over Cade's boot. He caught her, murmured in her ear, "You're doing fine," and moved away, the imprint of his arm scorching where it had touched. She'd said she'd stay the winter. With Cade around, she would never be cold.

Randi had managed to finish the last stanza without tripping over her feet or Cade's when a man came up to the two of them. He addressed Cade but he glared at her. "Is she the one?"

Cade grimaced and raked his hand through his hair. "Ned, this isn't the time or place."

"Anywhere's the time or place when someone's trying to break up my marriage," he returned.

Several of the people standing around listened curiously.

Realizing this man was Laura's husband, Randi extended her hand to him. "Hello, Mr. Thorn. I'm Miranda Sinclair."

He stared at her hand and scowled. "You want to get friendly? I don't think so."

"I don't want to get friendly, Mr. Thorn. I want to get reasonable, which is what you apparently haven't been."

Taken aback, Ned turned to Cade. "What are you gonna do about her? You said you were going to talk to her. Laura's planning on seeing her next week!" He looked anguished, scared and angry, all at the same time.

Cade took Ned's arm and guided him toward their table. He pointed to a chair. "Maybe we can get this straightened out."

Miranda crossed her arms over her chest. "I don't think so, gentlemen."

Cade frowned and gave her a warning look. "Randi…"

"I mean it, Cade. I'm advising Laura. I'm not

going to discuss anything with the two of you without her present.''

"She's not talking to me," Ned mumbled, pulling his hat low on his forehead. "And that's *your* fault."

"Get real, Mr. Thorn. If she's not talking to you, it's hardly my fault."

"If you hadn't put ideas in her head…"

"Laura has her own ideas, Ned," Randi said, feeling sorry for the young husband. But she suddenly had an idea herself—one Cade might not like. She faced him now, hoping he would go along with her. "I'd like to invite Laura and Ned to lunch tomorrow. Would you mind?"

"What are you doing, Randi?" His expression was wary.

"I just thought it would be nice if we had a neighborly lunch and we all got to know each other better."

Ned sat up straight. "Are you crazy?"

"No. I'm trying to help. If I call Laura and convince her to come, will you?"

Ned pushed his Stetson back and asked Cade, "Is she trying to pull something?"

Cade's gaze found hers and he searched—for honesty, for sincerity, for something she was afraid he wouldn't find. "I don't think so."

"Will you come?" Randi pressed.

"You'll call Laura?"

Randi nodded.

"What time?" Ned asked.

"One o'clock?"

"Fine." He pushed out of the chair, then said to Cade, "You'd better watch her. I think she has something up her sleeve. I know *I'll* be watching." With a lift of his brows, Ned Thorn crossed the room to the bar.

Cade watched his friend, then he looked into Randi's eyes. Hearing the strains of a ballad drift from the stage, he asked, "Would you care to dance?" He would much rather dance with her than argue with her. Maybe while they were dancing he could figure out what she was up to.

She studied him for a long moment. "I'd like that."

For a change he could read nothing in her expression or the tone of her voice. He wondered about the woman who was the lawyer; the woman he didn't know. They didn't touch until they stepped onto the dance floor.

Cade savored the sensation of bringing Randi close to him, of knowing he could hold her here safely with nothing getting out of hand. His arm surrounding her, his hand clasping hers, he guided her with gentle pressure she responded to easily. In his mind flashed a picture of another kind of dance, of naked bodies, Miranda responding—

"Do you think I have tricks up my sleeve?"

He sighed, sorry he had to banish the picture,

sorry he'd indulged in fantasy for even a moment. "I don't like getting mixed up in my neighbor's problems—at least, not this kind."

"Why not?"

She was pushing for more than a simple answer, but he didn't feel like digging into that place that still held so much anger. "Because it's none of my damn business! Now, do you want to argue or dance?"

Randi's blue eyes flashed. "I want to dance but I also want an answer to my question."

She was the most frustrating woman sometimes. Pushy, too, But he admired that about her; the way she spoke her mind and laid everything on the table. "I don't know if you have any tricks. I only know what you let me know and see. The woman who can take care of my sons so well might have an iron hide when it comes to practicing law."

"I see."

He heard it—that vulnerable tone that wasn't present often; only when he hurt her feelings. Susan had been good with tears and pouting but mostly cold silence when she didn't get the answer she wanted. But as he was coming to expect, Randi didn't stay silent.

Instead she challenged him. "So what you're saying is you question my ethics as a lawyer."

He'd stepped in quicksand and was sinking fast. Yet he knew that, unlike Susan, Randi wouldn't settle for anything less than complete honesty, either. "I'm not questioning your ethics. But I know how lawyers operate. And what you think is best for Laura might not be best for Ned or the two of them together. I won't be party to you splitting them up."

This time he saw the vulnerability in Randi's eyes and knew it was no act when she said, "I thought over lunch, maybe afterward, we could referee. If they both get out what's bothering them and someone helps them listen to each other, they might have a chance. That's it, Cade. No tricks."

He felt as low as the broken rail on the corral fence. And he didn't know what to say. He had to remind himself Miranda wasn't Susan. He'd misjudged his wife's character, her love for him, her desire for a family. Was he suspicious of all women now? Could Randi be as honest and sincere as she seemed?

He'd never meant to let bitterness, anger and distrust get a vise-like grip on his soul. But letting go of them wasn't easy. And he wasn't sure he should. They protected him and his sons from further betrayal and pain.

Instead of trying to smooth things over, he tightened his arm around Randi and brought her hand in to his chest.

She didn't go rigid against him as he might have expected. She never retaliated with viciousness. She didn't fight dirty. He rubbed his chin against her

temple, breathing in her fragrance, letting her softness seep into him, relishing the feel of a lovely
woman in his arms.

The other couples on the dance floor only made
it to the edge of Cade's consciousness. There wasn't
much room for anything or anyone other than him
and Randi. As they danced, her silk blouse slid
against his shirt, making him wonder if skin against
skin could have any more of an effect on his body.
His jeans created a friction against the smoother material of her slacks that caressed his thigh as they
moved.

When another couple bumped them and Randi's
breasts pressed against his chest, he felt her quick
intake of breath. Was dancing doing to her what it
was doing to him?

By the end of the song, he wanted to sling her
over his shoulder and carry her to the motel down
the street. But if he did, he would only be messing
with his sons' well-being. Although he might want
to bed Randi, he always put their welfare first. The
time in his life when he acted first and thought later
was long gone. Now, he didn't make a move without
examining all the consequences.

One dance stretched into another. Ballads gave
way to line dances and variations on the two-step.
Cade taught Randi, and they laughed and danced till
well after midnight. As they finally decided to call
it a night, Cade realized he'd never spent an evening

like this with Susan. After they'd arrived in Montana, he'd been occupied with learning everything about the ranch to make it a success. Susan had been frazzled by pregnancy and then Sean's care. She'd seen life as she'd known it slipping far away. Had he betrayed her by bringing her here?

It was the first time Cade had thought of their move like that, and it gave him pause.

As he drove back to the ranch, the wind howled. Randi had been as quiet as he had since they'd left the Round-Up. But now she commented, "It almost has a voice, doesn't it?"

Cade knew immediately what she meant. "A voice as high as the mountains and as wide as the valleys. Does it scare you?"

"A little," she murmured in the darkness. "But I imagine it becomes as much a part of the surroundings as the cottonwoods or the blue sky. I suppose it can be dangerous, though."

"Very dangerous when the temperatures drop. I'm just hoping snow doesn't come with it. At least, not for another week. Then we'll be ready for it."

Randi could count on one hand the pairs of headlights they'd passed since they left Hampton. She was city born and city bred, but something about this wide expanse of country called out to her. There was a simplicity about it and a peace she hadn't found anywhere else. She didn't find it isolating, but rather soul-filling. Now, the dark silent intimacy of sitting in the car with Cade was another matter entirely. It was exciting rather than peaceful, more dangerous than the winter wind.

She didn't know how it had happened so fast, but she'd fallen in love with Cade. She'd come to Montana, wondering if she could ever trust her judgment again. And now she knew she could. She'd thought a lot about what had gone wrong in New York. It hadn't started in New York.

Growing up without her mother, taking care of her brothers, wanting to earn her father's love and approval, she'd lost herself trying to please him. She needed to be loved for who she was, not what she did. Here, in Montana, she'd found another side of herself—a side that liked the country better than the city, a side that preferred the quiet over the bustle. She'd also learned to see a man for who and what he was.

She'd been blind to David's manipulation because she'd still wanted her father's approval. She'd believed her client because she hadn't dug deep enough. The bustle had been too loud, gaining success in her law firm too consuming, for her to look beyond the depositions and documents to see the truth.

Here, she could see clearly. And she could feel, too; feel more deeply than she'd ever felt before. She felt pulled toward Cade for so many reasons—his strength of character, his love for his sons, his juggling of their care and a life he believed in. If he could just drop the barriers, if he could just let go of the past hurt...

That was an awfully big "just."

Tonight while they were dancing, she'd felt his muscles grow taut when he'd held her close. She'd known he was aroused. But Cade was the epitome of control. In a way she was glad, but in another way she was disappointed. Although her head told her Cade's desire would never be enough, she wondered if it wouldn't be a good start, a way to break down some of his walls.

When they returned to the ranch, Cade stopped in front of the walk with the engine running. "I'm going to put this in the shed."

Randi hopped out and hurried to the porch with her head ducked. Charlie opened the door for her before her hand gripped the knob.

Inside, she unzipped her parka. "How are the boys?"

"Great night. Poker, videos, and cookies and milk. They stalled their bedtime and I let 'em." He grinned slyly.

She shook her finger at him. "You're a soft touch, Charlie. What is it about cowboys that makes them think they have to have such tough exteriors?"

"I don't think we're talkin' about me anymore."

Cade opened the door then, and Randi hung her parka on a wooden peg.

Charlie asked, "You two have a good time?"

Cade's gaze met Randi's. "The band was great."

Randi nodded. "Great."

Charlie arched his brows and motioned to the living room. "I lit the woodstove. It's almost burnt out. And I put extra blankets on the boys' beds." After he grabbed his coat from the rack, he set his hat on his head. "I'll see you tomorrow."

When Charlie closed the door behind him, Cade took off his hat and shrugged out of his coat. "Would you like a cup of hot chocolate before you turn in? It'll warm you up."

"I'd like that. Should I check on the boys?"

"Charlie usually tires them out. But if you want to check, go ahead."

Randi made sure all the boys were snug. She couldn't help but brush Sean's hair from his forehead. Tim cuddled a teddy bear close by his side. She adjusted the extra blanket over the bear. As she stood at Gregory's side, he opened his eyes. "You're home. I'm glad."

"I am, too," she murmured and pulled his blanket to his shoulders.

The eight-year-old closed his eyes and turned on his side.

When Randi returned downstairs, Cade sat on the sofa with two mugs of chocolate on the low table in front of him. "They're asleep?"

"Gregory opened his eyes for a few seconds."

Sitting beside Cade, she picked up the mug of chocolate.

Cade took a sip of his and set the mug on the table. "One Saturday night after I went into town, I looked in on them. They were asleep. In the middle of the night, I heard something and there was Gregory, watching me. When I asked what was wrong, he said he just wanted to make sure I'd come home."

"He's older than his years."

"Unfortunately, that's true. I've tried to make them feel secure, but I don't know if I've succeeded."

"They're secure, Cade. They know you're here for them."

"I don't want them to ever doubt it."

She heard what he wasn't saying. He didn't want them to ever think would leave like their mother had.

They sat sipping hot chocolate, listening to the wind whistle in the eaves, basking in the heat of the woodstove as it displaced any drafts.

Cade's knee brushed hers as he shifted toward her. "I did have a good time tonight."

She lifted her head and looked into his eyes. "So did I."

"It wasn't the theater and Sardi's."

"No, it was the Round-Up and dancing with you. And just as enjoyable." More enjoyable, if the truth be told, but she was afraid Cade would think she was exaggerating.

Cade reached out and tucked her hair behind her ear. "You're something to watch when you're dancing."

His thumb on the shell of her ear, his male scent mixed with the remnants of after-shave taunted her and sent her pulse racing. "What do you mean?"

He smiled—the way he did sometimes when Sean said something precocious. "You've got this great little wiggle."

She felt her cheeks color. "I don't wiggle. I dance."

"Remind me to videotape you sometime."

"Not a chance," she muttered.

"Do you know what I wanted to do all night?"

"What?" she asked breathlessly as his hand slipped beneath her hair and caressed her neck.

"Kiss you." He leaned toward her and touched his lips to hers, exploring, slipping from her lips to her cheek to her chin.

"You're so soft and smell so good," he murmured as his slight beard stubble rubbed her cheek, arousing her as much as his low words. Her heart lurched as his lips dawdled on her cheekbone. As his hands clasped her waist, his hot breath stirred the hair at her temple.

Cade brought his hands to her face and slowly slid his fingers through her hair, mesmerizing her with his brown eyes that glowed golden with desire. "You have such beautiful hair. All fire and glow. Like you."

With an inevitability she'd felt when they were dancing, when they'd stared into each other's eyes for the first time at the wedding, when he touched her, she accepted the crush of his mouth and the passion driving it. His tongue broke the seam of her lips. She reached for him, embracing Cade and his passion.

Deepening the kiss, he laid her back on the sofa, following her down. He tasted of chocolate and desire, potent and dangerous. But she wasn't afraid. Not of Cade nor of what was growing between them. She filled her arms with him as he filled her senses.

He drew her tongue into his mouth, then delved again into hers. She stroked his back, kneading her fingers into his muscles, discovering him.

For a moment, Cade let himself feast on Randi. He let his control slip so he could taste the passion, explore her depths, wedge his legs between hers. He could feel the softness of her through his jeans, and her welcoming arch when he pressed into her intensified his arousal. He enjoyed it as long as he could bear the pleasure. He tasted her until he was on the edge of finding release. He remembered loving a woman—and he froze.

Suddenly he realized that tempting himself was

one thing, making an irrevocable mistake was another. He was crazy to let his guard slip even a little.

He raised himself up, then planted his feet firmly on the floor.

Randi sat up. "Cade?"

She sounded a little lost and he knew exactly how she felt. "Some mistakes can be fixed. Some can't. I stopped before we made a mistake that can't be."

She slid her legs to the floor. "Why would it be a mistake?"

He raked his hands through his hair. "Because I have three sons sleeping upstairs who depend on me. Because you have a life in New York, because a vacation for you in Montana doesn't mean a damn thing."

"You seem so sure I want to go back to that life, that this is just a vacation. What if I want to stay?"

"For what? Six months? A year? Maybe two? If Susan couldn't stand it here, certainly a woman like you can't."

"A woman like me?"

"You have an established career!"

"And maybe I've been thinking about that career. Maybe I don't want to go back."

Cade shook his head, tormented by his doubts, the past. "It really doesn't matter if you do or you don't. Can't you understand, Randi? I could never ask you to stay. I will never do that again or expect a commitment."

Her blue eyes suddenly grew crystal clear and she understood. "You'll never love a woman again."

The words were slow in coming but they were firm and determined when he uttered them. "No, I won't."

Randi rose to her feet and stood before him, almost defiant in her posture. "You've made up your mind and as long as it's set, you *won't* love again."

Coming from her it sounded like a decree and a punishing sentence. "I have my sons. They're all I need."

"Maybe that's true, Cade. But they might need more than you can give them."

Anger rolled through him—that making the wrong choice years ago had left him with this legacy of distrust and anger at Randi because he still wanted her as desperately as he had a few minutes ago. "Go to bed, Miranda. Arguing about this won't change it."

She shook her head slowly. "No, arguing won't change it. The only thing that will is you letting go of the past and opening your heart. Good night, Cade."

She headed for her bedroom, her shoulders set, her back straight. Cade let her go, his gut twisting, his heart— Hell, nothing was going on with his heart. It had broken three years ago and hadn't felt anything but love for his sons since. That was what held it together. He wouldn't let Miranda Sinclair tamper with the uneasy peace he'd found.

Chapter Eight

The chaos in the kitchen rivaled the chaos in Randi's head. Tim, Gregory and Sean had the radio blasting as they played musical chairs. She wished she could expend her pent-up energy as easily. She and Cade had hardly spoken two sentences since she'd gone to bed last night. Early this morning he'd asked if she was going to call Laura. She'd answered that she was, then made the call. Cade had gone out to the barn.

Now he opened the door, found her wrist-deep in flour and his sons laughing and falling over the chairs. He frowned and said, "I'm going to change. Let me know if—"

The phone rang.

He turned down the radio and lifted the receiver.

Randi mixed the biscuits. She heard the pleasure in Cade's voice as he said, "Gavin! What's up?"

As Gavin explained, Cade listened. "Sure, you can stay for a couple of days. But you'll have to sleep in the bunkhouse or on the sofa. I've got a— Miranda Sinclair is here. She's been helping me with the boys.... Yeah, the maid of honor." After a pause, Cade mumbled, "I'll explain when you get here."

After Cade hung up, he came to the sink. "Gavin's at a conference in Denver. He's driving up at the end of the week."

"Does he visit often?"

"This'll be the first. He's been too busy getting his medical degree. He hasn't taken time off for anything in the past eight years. The last time I saw him before Jeff's wedding was a homecoming game at the college. Jeff, Nathan and I stayed the weekend, but Gavin only managed the day. I admire him. He did it all on his own. His father died when he was a kid and his mother passed away his first year in college. He's had it rough. But you'd never know it from his attitude or his determination."

Randi continued kneading the biscuit dough, trying to ignore Cade's broad shoulders, deep brown eyes and sensual lips as he stood beside her. He'd made himself explicitly clear last night, and she didn't want him to know that she'd been shaken by what had happened. "So Gavin's taking a vacation?"

"I'm not sure. It sounds more to me as if he just needs a few days to get away and think before he flies back to Norfolk where he's practicing now."

Randi didn't feel it was any of her business, so she didn't ask any more questions.

A truck rattled to a stop outside. Cade pushed back the curtain. "It's Laura and Ned. I'll be down in five minutes. By the way, Charlie said he'd watch the boys after lunch so we could have a little privacy."

"He knows about Laura and Ned?"

"He was there when Ned barged over, all upset. Charlie doesn't miss much."

Cade's shoulder brushed hers as he turned. His gaze collided with hers and held. Everything that had happened last night replayed in her mind, and she wished she could stop the aching in her heart.

"Five minutes," he said again, his voice husky.

She just nodded.

Luckily, Sean, Tim and Gregory chattered throughout the meal. Laura and Ned obviously weren't speaking—not to each other, anyway. After dessert, Cade took the boys to the bunkhouse.

Randi suggested, "Why don't we take our coffee to the living room. We'll be more comfortable."

"Thank you for lunch, Miss Sinclair. It was very good," Laura said as she perched on the edge of the sofa.

"Better than anything I've gotten lately at home," Ned muttered.

"Well, maybe if you'd help or pick up the babies when they cry, you'd get something besides sandwiches," Laura retorted.

"You'd just tell me I was doin' it wrong," Ned snapped.

Cade returned to the kitchen and threw his coat over a kitchen chair. When he entered the living room, Ned and Laura were glaring at each other.

Once Cade lowered himself into the wooden rocker, Randi said, "Why don't we get everything out in the open? Laura, you think you want a divorce. Why don't you tell Ned why."

"I've told him," she mumbled.

"You've told me zilch! Just that I'm not there for you. What does that mean?" The young rancher clenched his hands on the arms of the chair.

"It means I take care of Bobby and Gary all day and all night. Twenty-four hours a day. Sometimes they cry most of the day. When one stops, the other one starts. They nap at different times. And if I'm up and down in the middle of the night, too, I just feel so trapped." Her voice quivered. "I don't know what I'd do without Mom."

"Yeah, I know," Ned muttered.

Randi heard the dejection in Ned's voice and glanced at Cade.

Cade shifted in the rocker. "Laura, you know ranch life is tough. You grew up with it."

She pointed her finger at her husband. "He wanted the babies, too! They're *his* responsibility, too."

"You don't let me take responsibility," Ned retorted.

"How can you when you're never there! And then Saturday night you say you need a break and you go to the Round-Up. When do *I* get a break, let alone a solid night's sleep?"

"Maybe I'd help more if you acted like you want me around."

"I just told you I want you around!"

"No. You want me to take care of the twins. But when I do, you tell me I don't do it right. I don't feed 'em enough or I feed 'em too much. I pick 'em up too much or I don't pick 'em up enough. And you move away every time I touch you."

Silence echoed in the room until Laura finally broke it. "You only touch me when you want… when you want…" She glanced at Cade and Randi, obviously embarrassed to talk about it in front of them. Her voice went low. "If you'd just hug me, hold me at night, show me you care I'm your wife and the mother of your children…" Tears ran down the young woman's cheeks and she looked at her lap.

Cade looked terrifically uncomfortable. "Maybe

we should give them some time to talk on their own.''

Randi grabbed her mug. "Let's get a refill on the coffee." She followed Cade to the kitchen.

Going to the coffeepot, she warmed hers, then gestured with the pot.

Cade shook his head. "That's what you intended to do, isn't it?"

"I wanted to get them not only talking, but listening to each other. They've started to do that now."

"They have a lot of years in front of them," Cade commented.

"Yes, they do, and the only way they'll survive is to talk and listen, then talk and listen more."

He approached her slowly. "How did you get so smart?"

Pouring milk into her mug, she said, "I see it in the courtroom all the time. Witnesses have to talk. The judge and lawyers have to listen. Sometimes it's very rote. But other times, the truth inadvertently comes out. When I worked in legal aid, I was involved in lots of mediation to keep down court costs. People have to listen to each other before they can work anything out."

"Susan and I didn't talk enough, or listen, I guess. I never realized how much she opposed the move, how much she hated it here, until it was too late. She said her love had died and I didn't even know it.'' Cade rubbed his hand up and down the back of his neck. ''Even if I could have sold the ranch...''

''Would you have?''

''She didn't even give me the time to think about it. Just said she couldn't stand it here another day. *Trapped* was the word she used—like Laura.''

''But would you have moved back to New York to save your marriage?'' Randi pressed.

''I honestly don't know. I was committed to the ranch. It would have been difficult to give up the dream. But if she had given me the slightest bit of hope, I would have tried. Maybe I could have let Charlie run the place. But Susan wasn't looking for a compromise.''

''Were you?'' It was dangerous territory but it was somewhere Randi felt she had to go.

Cade's eyes narrowed and his tone became curt. ''I would have worked to keep my marriage to-gether—for the boys' sake if for no other reason.'' Pulling out a chair at the kitchen table, he sat. ''I've been thinking about our...talk last night. I'll under-stand if you feel you can't stay.''

Randi had spent a sleepless night thinking about their ''talk.'' She loved Cade, and if she stayed he might see that. But if he'd truly hardened his heart, her love might not make a bit of difference. All she could do was hope that more time would show Cade that love could heal instead of cause pain.

Suddenly the kitchen door opened, and Sean,

Timothy, Gregory, and Charlie plowed in. Snow dusted their coats.

"It's snowin', Dad, and Charlie says it's gonna be an early whopper," Tim informed them.

Cade went to the door and looked out. "It's coming down hard and fast."

Charlie removed his Stetson and ran the brim through his fingers. "I know you like to do things in your own time. But my bones tell me this could be bad."

Cade thought about the situation for a few moments. "All right. Let's get feed to those cows. There's no sense trying to move them in this. Have you talked to Al and Buck yet?"

"They're already filling the bed of the pickup," Charlie said with a wink.

Cade clapped the old man on the shoulder, the bond of affection between them obvious. "I want to make sure everything's secure here before I leave. Give me fifteen minutes."

Charlie nodded. "You got it. I'll drive."

"Now, Charlie…"

"Don't you 'Charlie,' me. The more hands, the faster this will go."

Randi could see Charlie's determination as well as Cade's concern. She helped Sean out of his coat. "Don't worry about us. We'll be fine."

"If the wind picks up, the electricity could go out. It's happened," Cade warned her.

"What do you do?"

"Keep the woodstove stocked. Lanterns are in the basement. Candles are in the cupboard in the downstairs bathroom."

"I can get a lantern, Dad," Gregory offered.

"That would be a big help."

Laura and Ned came into the kitchen. Ned said, "We'd better get home. We saw it snowin' out the window."

Laura approached Randi. "Thanks for lunch and all."

Randi sensed a definite decrease in tension between Laura and Ned. "You're welcome."

The young wife gave her a tentative smile. "I... uh...don't think I'll be needing your services. But maybe I could just call and talk sometime?"

"Sure."

Ned addressed Randi, too. "I'm sorry I gave you such a tough time last night."

"I understand, Ned. Really, I do."

He helped his wife into her coat. She looked up at him with a smile that said they'd begun to work out their problems.

After they left for their truck, Cade said, "I'll bring in a good load of firewood before I leave. It might be pretty late when we get back."

Randi was thankful for his concern, but she was able-bodied. "I know where it is. I can always bring in more."

He looked surprised for a moment but recovered quickly. "Keep the lights blazing. It'll make it easier for us to get back."

"If the electricity goes out, I'll make sure we put the lanterns in the windows," she assured him.

A strange light shone in his eyes—one of admiration mixed with desire. She felt herself respond to the desire.

Cade's gaze fell to her lips, to the pulse at her throat. Then he beckoned to his sons. "You can get your sleeping bags out of your closet in case you need to sleep downstairs. I have to find my long underwear. Let's get cracking."

Randi went to the cupboard for a thermos as she heard him climb the stairs with his sons. Her heart beat fast, as she thought about Cade driving into a snowstorm. She had to just keep telling herself he knew what he was doing. Now all she had to do was believe it.

Cade returned to the kitchen wearing several layers, a long coat of some kind thrown over his arm. "I said goodbye to the boys. They're deciding what games they want to play with you tonight."

She offered him the thermos. "I can brew more for the others...."

"Charlie's taking care of that. He knows the drill." Cade slipped into the duster that made him seem even taller, more powerfully masculine, more...everything. Then he took the thermos.

"Do you have any idea when you'll be back?"

"We'll have to come back for a second load. It depends how fast the temperature drops and how heavy the snow gets." He must have seen the worry in her eyes because he crossed over to her with a gentle look on his face. "I'll be all right. Are you sure you don't mind being here alone? I could convince Charlie to stay—"

"No. We'll be fine. Don't *you* worry. Take care of yourself." Her voice wobbled slightly.

He tilted his head. "Randi…"

"I care about you, Cade. I can't help worrying."

He brushed his hand along her cheek. He looked as if he was going to say something, but he didn't. And he didn't kiss her, either, although she glimpsed the longing in his eyes. He stepped away, picked up his hat and left. Randi peered out the door window until he disappeared into the barn. How could she convince him love was worth taking a risk? How could she convince him that she would like nothing more than to be his wife and a mother to his sons?

In order not to worry the boys, Randi tried to stay away from the windows. Whenever she looked out, she couldn't keep the stab of worry from turning into fear. She didn't want Sean, Tim and Gregory to see her fear.

After supper, they helped her clean up. As Gregory wiped off the table, he asked, "Are you gonna sleep upstairs in Dad's bed tonight?"

She'd spent one night in Cade's bed and had dreamed vivid dreams of him and her....

"It's warmer down here," Tim said. "And you don't hear the wind so much. Maybe we could sleep with you."

With Cade gone, the boys needed to still feel secure. She could help with that. Smiling, she said, "I don't think we'd all fit in my bed. But we could bring your sleeping bags down here. We can sleep near the woodstove and be plenty warm."

"You mean it?" Sean asked with a wide grin.

"Sure. We'll make popcorn, tell stories, and I'll teach you a new card game."

"So the night goes fast," Gregory deduced.

"Yep. Before you know it, it will be bedtime."

"Dad got out his sleeping bag for you in case you need it. Should I go get it?"

"Go get all of them, then we'll be set."

Keeping the boys occupied wasn't so difficult. As the snow piled up, Sean's eyelids drooped. After a final hand of fish, they moved from the kitchen table to the floor in the living room. Randi sat with Sean tucked in by her right arm, Tim sitting on her left. Gregory sat propped against the sofa. She read to them from one of their favorite books every night now. Cade always stayed on the corner of Sean's bed, watching her.

As she finished the story and closed the book, she wondered where he was, if he was safe.

Gregory seemed to read her mind. "The snow's gettin' deeper. Do you think Dad's okay?"

She didn't know and she couldn't lie. When man braved the elements, anything could happen. "I think your dad and Charlie and the others know what they're doing and will take care of each other. Don't you?"

All three boys nodded.

After she settled the boys in their sleeping bags, she went to the kitchen to make a cup of tea. And to wait. She tried to read, but couldn't help going to the window every so often. The snow, wind, and lack of visibility didn't reassure her.

She changed into a jogging suit instead of her nightgown. She'd only brought the cotton one, and the wind whipping around the corner of the kitchen made it drafty despite the heat filtering in from the living room.

Around midnight, she thought she heard something—heavy steps on the porch. She pulled open the door, the wind pelting her with snow as she did. Cade appeared before her, and she stepped aside so he could come in. He looked tired, worn-out, wet, and stiff.

He stripped off his gloves, doffed his hat, and closed his eyes for a moment. "I was never so glad to see the lighted windows."

She wanted to hug him and kiss him and tell him how much she loved him, but with the boys around the corner, not knowing how Cade would react, she said, "I'll heat up some soup. Coffee's been waiting for you."

He opened his eyes then, his gaze skimming over her blue jogging suit. "You should be sleeping."

She might not be able to tell him she loved him, but she wasn't going to hide her feelings, either. "I couldn't sleep until I knew you were safe."

Breaking eye contact with her, he tried to unknot the bandanna around his throat, but swore when he couldn't.

She didn't hesitate to help him. "Let me."

He stood perfectly still as she brought the knot to the side of his neck. "My fingers are too stiff," he mumbled.

When her hot fingers brushed against the cold of his neck, she felt him start. "You've got to get out of this stuff into dry clothes. How's Charlie?"

"I made him stay in the pickup while Al, Buck and I dropped the feed."

"Didn't you warm up in the truck?"

"I stayed in the back coming home."

Now, she understood. Only three of them could fit into the cab. Cade must have taken the last shift on the open bed of the pickup.

Finally, the knot came loose. But instead of moving away, she unbuttoned his coat. "Do you have any liquor?"

He gave her a strange look. "Top cupboard in the back."

"We'll put some in the coffee."

He let her unbutton the long coat, but when she went to help him out of it, he growled, "I can do it."

"Yes, I'm sure you can. But you don't have to." She helped him free his arms despite his scowl.

"Do you want to help undress me, too?" he asked, his voice low and raspy.

"It might not be a bad idea. Need help with your boots?"

He rolled his eyes and she thought a small smile twitched his lips. "No, but I'm going to the bathroom to shed all this so I don't drag the snow upstairs."

"I can get your robe for you. Pajamas..."

"I don't wear pajamas. The robe's fine."

Randi knew he wasn't going to let her do much, that was for certain.

While he headed for the bathroom, she poured a good shot of whiskey into a mug of coffee, then went upstairs for his robe. The bathroom door was shut when she brought the robe downstairs so she rapped softly on the door.

He opened it. His chest was bare, but he still wore his jeans. "I'm too beat to eat. The coffee is all I need. You can go to bed now if you want. I'm going to lie on the sofa and try to warm up.''

''You just get dry. I'll get the coffee.''

Despite Cade's protest that he wasn't hungry, she warmed up the soup anyway and put it into another mug. Then she took it and the coffee to the living room. Tim, Sean and Gregory were still sound asleep.

Cade came in, saw the two mugs, and sat on the sofa beside her. ''You don't listen, do you?''

She felt the brush of terry as he sat. Noticing his bare feet, she pulled the afghan from the back cushions and drew it over their laps. ''I listen. And then I do what I think is best. You need as much warmth as you can get. A little nourishment thrown in won't hurt.''

Cade sipped at the coffee. Then he sat back with the soup, ate it with a spoon, and drank the broth. When he set the mug on the coffee table, he asked in a low voice, ''Are you satisfied?''

''Are you warm yet?'' she returned.

''No. The soup might have warmed my insides but the rest of me doesn't know it yet.''

She felt him shiver against her. She could take a risk or she could give him another cover and play it safe. Suddenly, playing it safe didn't feel like living.

She stood and ordered in a whisper, ''Lie back.''

''Randi…'' he warned in a low voice that vibrated through her.

"Everyone knows body heat is the best way to warm up. Just move over to the back of the sofa, and I'll lie beside you for a few minutes until you get warm." She could almost hear the snow falling in the silence.

Either Cade was very cold or just too tired to fight her because he wedged himself against the back of the sofa. When she curled up beside him, nestling her head into his shoulder, he pulled the afghan over them.

Cade called himself every kind of fool for giving in to temptation. But he was so damn cold, he couldn't resist Randi's offer. He knew she was right about body heat. The sooner he warmed up, the sooner he'd fall asleep. Saturday night, after he'd told her he would never love another woman, he'd tossed and turned till dawn. Lack of sleep was catching up.

Lying stiff along the back of the sofa, he realized how soft and pliant Randi was against him. If he relaxed, he'd get warm a lot quicker. Inhaling a deep breath, he told himself she was just a warm body. But he didn't believe it. Miranda Sinclair had gotten under his skin in so many ways.

She acted like a mother to his sons and didn't seem to resent a bit of it. Unlike Susan, who had hated taking care of the boys when they were sick, constantly hiring baby-sitters so she could go shopping, or play tennis, or meet with friends. He'd understood she needed to get out. But she'd seemed to like getting out more than spending time with their sons.

She'd loved going to cocktail parties with Cade to make business contacts and find new clients. *He* had hated it. His job as a stockbroker had always been a means to an end. Susan had always seemed to concentrate more on everything else than on him—on their family. He should have seen the warning signals.

Randi seemed to thrive here. She focused on the boys as if she'd been doing it all her life. She was genuinely friendly with Al and Buck and Charlie, and they liked her. Susan had kept her distance from them and they'd kept their distance from her.

Randi's arm slipped across Cade's chest. He sucked in a breath. Then he realized her breathing was even and deep. She'd fallen asleep.

He curved his arm around her to keep her on the sofa, to keep her safe. When she'd opened that door tonight…he'd felt as if he'd come home. And that was crazy. This had been home for five years.

His feelings were sentimental hogwash—home, hearth, a wife waiting. It was time for a reality check. Randi had been here five weeks. She still didn't realize what ranch life was all about. It might be a diversion for now, but as he reminded himself over and over, she was city born and bred. Besides, how could a family compare to the prestigious career waiting for her in New York?

She brushed her cheek against his robe and he almost forgot about reality all over again. He might be cold but some parts were thawing out mighty fast! Closing his eyes, he willed himself into sleep.

At first light, Cade opened his eyes. He was holding on to Randi as if he had the right. She fit against him too perfectly and he was aroused again. Even in sleep she had a power over him.

He moved his hand from where it had settled near her breast and murmured her name.

She opened her eyes and smiled. "I guess I fell asleep."

"You should move to the sleeping bag or your bed. It would be better if the boys don't see us like this."

Her smile vanished. "Better for your sons or better for you?"

"Better for all of us," he growled, frustrated because he'd like nothing better than to keep her exactly where she was.

Quickly, Randi sat up, slid from the sofa and crawled into her sleeping bag. Then she turned her back to him.

Cade swore under his breath. The least he could have done was thank her.

The problem was, it was getting more and more difficult to push her away.

Chapter Nine

The following Sunday afternoon, the sun glistened on the four to six inches of snow that hadn't yet melted. Randi opened the oven, removing the last two baking sheets dotted with chocolate-chip cookies. Having another male around dipping into the snacks made a difference.

As if on cue with her thoughts, the door opened and Gavin, Sean, Tim and Gregory blustered in. Snow slid from their coats, boots, and gloves.

"You look as if you guys are the snowmen," Randi observed.

Gavin shed his coat and gloves, then pulled off his boots, setting them behind the door on a rug Randi had laid there for that purpose. "These three are tough. They throw mean snowballs."

One thing Randi had noticed about Gavin immediately was his affinity with the boys. She should have guessed he would relate well to children since he specialized in pediatrics. He'd arrived late Friday. As tall as Cade, with black hair and gray eyes that seemed to take in more than the obvious, he came across as a confident, handsome man who could make conversation easily and was always ready with a smile. There was a kindness about him that was easy to respond to. Yet, she sensed a preoccupation bothering him when he thought no one was watching. She suspected it was the reason he'd come to visit Cade.

As Randi helped the boys with their coats, she said, "They not only throw mean snowballs, but they also roll in the snow and get all wet. Upstairs, guys, and change. Take your wet clothes down to the basement."

After a few grumbles and grumps, they charged up the stairs.

Gavin chuckled. "I'll bet they keep you stepping."

She hung Sean's coat beside Gregory's. "The secret is to stay one step ahead."

Gavin studied her.

Feeling self-conscious, she asked, "What?"

He shrugged. "You seem so different here than when I met you at the wedding."

She flipped her ponytail over her shoulder and

crossed to the baking sheets to remove the cookies.
"It must be the hairstyle."

"It has nothing to do with hairstyle or clothes.
You love those boys, don't you?"

This was Cade's friend, a former fraternity buddy.
She had better be very careful. "Who wouldn't?"

He came up beside her and motioned toward the
cookies. "Mind if I have one?"

"Take two. Once the boys and Cade hit them,
there won't be many left." She slipped the turner
under another one and lifted it to the rack. "How
do you like sleeping in the bunkhouse?" If she kept
the conversation focused on him, it would be safer.

"It reminds me of dorm life, before I moved to
the frat house and had my own room."

"Did you and Cade have classes together?" She'd
never talked to Cade about his life before New York.

"No. He was my big brother during pledging. He
was two years ahead of me."

"I didn't realize that."

"He and Jeff graduated together. Nathan and I
graduated two years later."

"Did Cade go straight to New York after gradu-
ation?"

"Actually, he went sooner. He served an internship there. His grades were exceptional and his fi-
nance professor took notice. He'd worked on Wall
Street himself. Anyway, he got Cade a shot at the

internship and the rest is history. Cade has always excelled at anything he's tried.''

Randi nodded. "Including being a father and running this ranch. I can't believe his ex-wife just left and—" She stopped before she said too much.

Gavin slowly ate one of the cookies. "I met Susan. Once. Cade brought her back to the college for homecoming."

Randi removed the remainder of the cookies.

He ate the second cookie, then lounged against the counter watching her. "Well? Aren't you going to ask me what I thought of her?"

"It's none of my business."

He gave her a knowing smile. "I think it's very much your business if the way you look at Cade is any indication. Not to mention the way he looks at you. You two could start a fire without matches or two sticks to rub together."

Randi realized there was no point in hiding her feelings from Gavin since he'd obviously guessed what they were. "What *did* you think of her?"

He didn't hesitate for an instant. "I thought she was too shallow for a man who feels as deeply as Cade. And I was right."

"Because of her..." Randi wasn't quite sure how to put it.

"Cade won't let you get close," Gavin finished.

"Only close enough that it hurts not to be able to get closer," she murmured.

"You love him as much as you love the boys."

Unable to deny it, and not wanting to, she nodded and tears came to her eyes. "You must think I'm crazy. I only met him at the wedding." She turned away, lifting more cookies onto the rack.

Gavin clasped her elbow. "I don't think you're crazy. I know how fast love can happen and how devastating it is when there are obstacles."

She could see he really did understand, and she could also see a deep pain in his eyes as if he had loved and maybe lost.

The door opened. Before Randi could react, Cade was standing in the kitchen, staring at Gavin's hand on her arm. She pulled away.

Cade's gaze raked her up and down, then settled on Gavin. "I thought you had plans to build snowmen."

"Did that. The boys went upstairs to change."

"Long ago?"

"Just a few minutes," Randi answered. "I'll go check and see if they need help." She could feel Cade's gaze on her back as she left the kitchen.

Anger shook Cade as he opened the refrigerator and lifted the carton of milk. Gavin was a friend— a good friend, he reminded himself. Then why in blazes had he been touching Randi?

Cade plunked the milk on the table and went to the cupboard for a glass.

"Is something wrong?" Gavin asked.

"No. Nothing's wrong. Everything's dandy." The last of the cows had been moved to winter pastures, and Randi and Gavin seemed to get along like two old friends. Just dandy.

"You know, Cade, I'm no stranger to work. Is there something around here I can do to help?"

Cade felt guilty for the anger. He had no hold on Randi. And Gavin was free to start anything he wanted with whomever he pleased. He'd had no time to even think about dating the past eight years. He'd been studying and working too many hours of each day since Cade had met him as a fraternity pledge.

"I have to ride out tomorrow and check the protein blocks in the winter pastures. But there's wood to split," Cade told him.

"Splitting logs could be exactly what I need."

Ever since Gavin had arrived, Cade could tell his friend was mulling something over. "How long's it going to take till you tell me why you came?"

Gavin took another glass from the cupboard. "I have a decision to make."

"Decisions have never been a problem for you. You've always known what you wanted." Cade had always admired Gavin's single-minded determination.

"I submitted a proposal to work with a pediatrician in Denver who's studying developmental problems in children."

"Is that what you want?"

Gavin shrugged. "It's an option. But so is taking over a pediatrician's practice in Four Oaks. It's temporary but he's thinking about retiring."

The town sounded familiar. Cade suddenly realized why. "Four Oaks, Virginia? Isn't that where Jessie Windsor came from?"

"Man, do you have a memory!"

"What I remember is your letter to me after you broke up with her."

"She's still there and she's not married," his friend explained.

Cade poured milk for both of them. "You want to give it another try?"

"I want to give it *a* try. We never had a chance the first time around."

Cade took a few cookies from the rack and sat at the table. "I hope you're not asking me for advice."

"A few thoughts on the subject wouldn't hurt." Gavin pulled out the chair across from Cade.

"I think you ought to do what your gut tells you to do, no matter what anyone else thinks or says."

Gavin lowered himself into the chair. "But you believe I should let the past alone, don't you?"

"I believe the past can be a force as powerful as the present. You deal with it as best you can. I don't want to revisit mine. But you might have to. You came here to think. So think. And maybe by the time you're ready to leave, you'll have an answer." Cade hoped Gavin would have an easy time finding his answer. Then, at least one of them would.

As Sean sat beside Randi on his bed, he flipped to the next page of the book she was reading before bedtime. Cade sat at the foot of Tim's bed, propped against the post, his long legs crossed at the ankles.

When the phone rang, Cade said, "Gavin will get it. Doctors automatically pick up."

Randi didn't know what to make of Cade's mood. Ever since last Sunday night when she'd slept in his arms, he'd kept more distance than was usual even for him. Gavin's presence seemed to increase the tension, rather than relieve it.

Gavin's voice came soaring up the stairs. "Randi, it's for you."

Cade dropped his legs to the floor. "I'll finish the book. You go ahead."

She squeezed Sean's shoulders and kissed him on the forehead. "I'll see you in the morning." Then she crossed to Tim and Gregory. "Oatmeal or eggs for breakfast?"

"Eggs," they both chorused.

She smiled and gave each of them a hug, then, with Cade's gaze boring into her back, went downstairs and picked up the phone in the kitchen.

"Miss Sinclair, it's Laura. I don't want to keep you. I just wanted to tell you…well…things are better. Much better."

"I'm glad to hear that."

"Ned's been helping me more with the twins, and I'm trying to let him do it his way. And…well…last night we went to the Round-Up. Mom kept the boys. It was like before we were married. We danced…we kissed…and when we got home, the babies even co-operated by sleeping through the night."

Randi could easily read between the lines.

"So, I just wanted to thank you."

After Randi assured Laura that no thanks were necessary, she said good-night, hung up the phone, and turned to find Gavin watching her intently.

"Charlie tells me you fit in real well around here," he remarked.

"I didn't think Charlie gossiped."

"It wasn't gossip. Just a statement of fact."

"All that matters is what Cade thinks."

"If he asked you to stay, would you stop practicing law?"

"I've been thinking about it. What I'd really like to do is open a practice in Hampton and charge reasonable rates. Maybe specialize in mediation. Wouldn't that be a switch?"

Gavin grinned. "It certainly would be."

She shook her finger at him. "Lawyers do do some good in this world."

He laughed. "I'm not a hard sell, Randi."

She frowned. "No. But Cade is. How can I get him to believe in love again?"

Gavin capped her shoulder. "Just give him some time."

"I'm afraid time won't do it. And if it doesn't, the boys will get hurt worst of all. I can't let that happen, yet I'm not sure what to do."

The understanding silence between them was broken by Cade's deep voice. "This is the second time today I feel as if I'm interrupting something," he said from the doorway.

Gavin moved away from Randi. "You're not interrupting anything." He took his coat from the rack. "Since I'll be up at the crack of dawn, I'm turning in."

"You don't have to leave on my account," Cade snapped. "Maybe I'm the one who should turn in."

Gavin opened the door. "Or maybe you and Randi should talk. I'll see you in the morning."

After Gavin shut the door, Cade approached her. "Is that what you want to do? Talk? Or do you have something else in mind? Maybe you were putting the moves on Gavin."

Randi had never seen Cade's face so hard, the line of his mouth so harsh. "That was an insult, Cade, to both me and Gavin."

He put an arm on either side of her, propping his hands on the counter. "Maybe so. But I want to know if it's true."

His size, and the anger she sensed brewing in him, should have intimidated her. But they didn't—because this was Cade. "You don't want to know if it's true. You want to use any excuse you can find to push me away. Admit it, Cade, you're afraid of me and what I make you feel." As soon as she said it, she saw the flash of desire in his eyes, the emotions he couldn't deny.

Then all of it disappeared as he yanked her against him and kissed her with all the pent-up passion he'd been holding in check. The tumultuous kiss was more combative than seductive, more explosive than expert, more raw and anguished than urgent and coaxing. Her palms settled on his flannel shirt as if to hold back the power and the pain.

The kiss was filled with darkness rather than light—all the unanswered questions, all the longing, all the distrust. She could taste Cade's distrust and doubts as well as his desire. He didn't want to want her. He didn't want to feel anything for her. Maybe that was why she'd goaded him, hoping he would open his eyes and his heart to all the possibilities between them.

She burned for him and felt him burning for her. And the sexual heat flamed out of control. He plunged his tongue into her mouth, then swept her into his arms and carried her to her bedroom.

He didn't turn on the light but laid her on the bed and came down beside her. Before she could breathe, let alone think, he covered her mouth with his again. His hand slid under the band of her sweatshirt and foraged until he found her breast. She moaned when his fingers slid over her. She'd wanted his touch, she'd waited for his touch for so long. Primitive desire rose, tearing at her, demanding satisfaction.

Filling her hands with his shirt, she pulled it from his jeans. Her palms met hot, taut skin and as she raked her nails across his back, he shuddered. In a split second, he pushed her bra above her breasts while he continued to ravish her mouth. Lightning burst inside her, spreading tingles to her fingers and toes, pulling tighter and tighter the tension gathering in her womb.

Cade intended to possess. She'd seen jealousy in his eyes when he'd noticed Gavin's hand on her arm, his fingers capping her shoulder. In some ways Cade was as elemental as the land he loved. But did the jealousy come strictly from passion or from the feelings behind it?

Cade's hands branded her as he moved his thigh over her leg. His lips broke away to string kisses down her neck, to find her breast. His tongue was rough on her nipple, the insides of his lips were like velvet. The combination arched her back and urged her to lace her hands in his hair. Her heart pounded so hard she could barely hear her thoughts. And she didn't care. All she wanted to do was love Cade and show him how much she wanted to be a part of his life.

He left one breast and found the other. His hand went to the waist of her sweatpants and eased inside.

But he didn't hurry to touch her intimately. He let his hand rest there as he again possessed her mouth, thrusting and withdrawing, thrusting and withdrawing, conveying exactly what he wanted to do next.

All she could do was accept and give back— stroke and caress—so that he knew she wanted him as much as he wanted her. She wanted him to fill her. She wanted him to love her.

When he broke away again, he sucked in a deep breath. "You understand what's happening here, don't you, Miranda? I want you. You want me. And we're going to satisfy the itch that's been dogging both of us."

Cade's words didn't belong with the kisses and the touches. She wasn't sure they even belonged to Cade. He was using them now to push her away even as he touched her still with an intimacy borne from more than a sexual itch. "I understand what's happening. You want to have sex instead of making love. The line's not that straight or clear, Cade."

"I know exactly which side of the line I'm on, and you'd better get it straight, too."

Sliding away from his hands, his touch, from the feelings he wouldn't embrace, she propped herself against the headboard. "I know which side of the line I'm on, Cade. I love you. But your heart's not accepting any love, is it?"

In the darkness of the bedroom, his voice was a hoarse whisper as he sat up. "I don't believe in anything I can't see, touch, or feel."

"You could see, touch and feel my love if you'd let yourself."

Cade's silence vibrated in the bedroom. Finally he responded, "You think what you want, Randi. I'm not going to sugarcoat the truth or call something love when it's sex, when it's lust, when it's desire."

Hot tears burned her eyes, and she was thankful he couldn't see them in the dark. All she had left was a little bit of pride. She wouldn't plead with him to accept something he wouldn't believe in. The mattress shifted as he got to his feet.

As he opened the bedroom door, light spilled in from the hall. Then the door closed and the sound of it latching echoed in the stillness of the room.

Randi let the tears fall, not knowing how to stop them, not wanting to. She wouldn't keep the hurt inside so it could eat away at her the same way Cade's pain ate at him. She couldn't heal him. She could only love him. He would have to find the courage to heal himself.

Cade had avoided Randi at breakfast by claiming he'd grab a cup of coffee at the bunkhouse and get an early start. It wasn't a solution, but it gave him more time to think, more time to sort out what had happened last night and the reason for the tight feeling in his chest that he'd experienced since he'd shut Randi's bedroom door.

Now, as he entered the kitchen before supper, he

saw her and vividly remembered the time in her bed all over again.

She topped a large pot with a lid and said, "I sent the boys upstairs for a few minutes. There's something I have to tell you."

His heart pounded faster.

"I received a phone call this afternoon. My law firm called. They have a case they need my input on. They want me to fly back as soon as I can."

Cade felt as if he'd been roped, tied and branded. "What did you tell them?"

"That I needed twenty-four hours and I'd get back to them tomorrow."

Self-defense was the best offense. "I guess your vacation's over. Don't worry about me and the boys. We'll be fine. In fact, the last time Charlie was in Hampton, a waitress at the café asked him if I still needed a housekeeper. She has the name of someone who's interested."

"I told you I'd stay the winter," Randi said softly.

"And I told you we'd take one day at a time. I never expected you to stay. We both knew you had a career to go back to."

Randi just looked at him as if waiting for something. He didn't have anything else to say. "I'm going to wash up. Then I'll tell the boys."

Cade didn't even unbutton his jacket but headed for the stairs, convincing himself that this turn of events was for the best. For everyone.

Chapter Ten

Tim, Gregory and Sean came racing down the stairs. Sean ran to Randi and wrapped his arms around her legs. "We don't want you to go."

She crouched down to Sean's level, not knowing what to say. She'd hoped beyond hope that Cade would ask her to stay. But after last night, she should have known better; she should have realized the call from New York would give him the excuse he needed to send her packing. But now, how was she supposed to deal with these three little boys she'd come to love as much as she loved their father?

Gregory stood beside his brother. "Dad says you're leaving tomorrow or the day after."

"He's right," she admitted, trying to keep her voice from shaking. It was obvious Cade couldn't wait to get rid of her. She didn't want to prolong the pain of goodbye, either. Maybe she should take the first flight out.

"We need you here," Tim said with an expression as sad as his brothers'.

Randi had no idea how to explain, so she put it in the simplest terms she could. "I care about you very much. I care about your dad, too. But he doesn't care for me in the same way. So it hurts for us to be together. Maybe if I go back to New York, we'll stop hurting."

"It's not fair," Tim said angrily.

"No, it's not fair," Randi agreed. "You're going to find lots of things in life aren't fair. But you know what? We can always be friends, even if I'm not here. I'll write to you. And you can write to me."

"I can't write," Sean complained with tears in his eyes.

"I know you can't. But you can draw me pictures. Okay?"

He nodded and clung a little tighter.

"Can you come back and visit?" Tim asked hopefully.

"Probably not soon. But maybe sometime. Maybe you can come visit me. And I'll tell you what. Why don't we try to make tonight special? The three of you decide what you'd like to do most and that's what we'll do."

"I want to play cards," Tim suggested.

"I want to eat popcorn and watch movies," Gregory protested.

"*I* want to read stories," Sean argued.

"Maybe we can fit in all three. Let's get dinner on the table, then we can get started." She was going to remember every moment of tonight as vividly as she could. She might be sorry later, but for now she needed a special night as much as they did.

Cade rode Storm long and hard, racing the wind, pounding over the last of the snow, hoping the cold would numb his mind as well as his body. But nothing helped. Not long rides. Not working till he dropped. Not spending time with his sons who mentioned Randi in every other breath.

She'd been gone a week. The longest week of his life.

When Susan had left, he'd been numb, in shock. But taking care of his sons had eased the pain, had filled empty hours, had given him reason enough to go on. Since Randi left, nothing eased the ache, the longing, the niggling sensation that he'd lost something far more precious than he'd realized.

The same day Randi made the call to her law firm to tell them she was returning, she'd gotten a flight out. So had Gavin. He'd driven her to the airport. Neither of them had said much to Cade, but Cade realized that was his own fault for having acted like a bear. But that last night had been sheer torture—

playing a few rounds of crazy eights, watching a video, listening to Randi read his sons a story for the last time.

Cade slowed Storm to a trot and guided him to the first spot on the ranch where he'd kissed Randi. Dismounting, he held Storm's reins as he stared at the snow-banked stream. His breath puffed white and as he inhaled, the cold air seared his lungs.

And then Jeff and Katie had called with their news. They were expecting a baby in June.

Cade was thrilled for them. He knew the joy of children—unequaled joy when a couple truly wanted a child. But after the call, all he could think about was Randi. He could picture her pregnant with his baby....

Was it more than a resurrected dream?

He and Randi had connected at the wedding in some elemental way. He'd called it "mutual attraction."

She'd taken to his sons like a woman who missed having children of her own. He'd called that "luck."

She'd taken to riding as if she belonged in a Western saddle. He'd called that "coincidence."

She'd said she loved him. He'd called that "lust."

She could have stayed.

After what you did to her? You threw her love back in her face!

Why?

Because of Susan. Because of the past. Because he *was* afraid to try again.

Fear.

For the past three years, he'd been hanging on to anger and bitterness and a sense of betrayal, thinking they would protect his heart, prevent him from giving his soul. But somehow Randi had seen below the surface and confronted him with the truth—a truth he hadn't been ready to hear.

And now he'd lost her. He'd never been very good at saying he was sorry, and he doubted if she'd want to hear it.

Setting his foot in the stirrup, he mounted Storm and headed for home.

At one o'clock in the morning, Cade still couldn't asleep. He'd put the boys to bed, watched television, tried to work on the computer. His lack of concentration accomplishing little, he'd gone to bed. And stared at the ceiling for the past hour.

A floorboard creaked and he was on instant alert. It could be one of his sons going to the bathroom. It could be something else. If one of them wasn't feeling well…

"Dad?"

He sat up. "What is it, Gregory?"

The eight-year-old crawled up onto the bed with him. "I can't sleep."

"Why?"

"I miss Randi."

Cade switched on the bedside lamp. "So do I."

"Really?"

"Well, sure. I got used to her being here, too."

"Oh."

Something was on Gregory's mind. "Don't you believe I miss her?"

"She said you don't care as much for her as she cares for you. She said if she stayed, you'd both hurt. Why?"

Cade had wondered what Randi had told his sons. He should have known she'd tell them the truth. "Do you understand what it means to trust someone?"

"You mean, like I trust you to make sure I don't drown when I'm swimmin'?"

"That's right. Sometimes it's hard to trust people. I trusted your mom and she left us. I was afraid if I trusted Randi, she'd leave, too."

"*You* were afraid?"

"Yep." He suddenly remembered what Randi had advised him about sharing his weaknesses with his sons. Maybe it wasn't so difficult, after all.

"But she *did* leave," Gregory stated morosely.

"If I had asked her, I think she would have stayed. But I don't know for sure because I didn't ask. I couldn't ask her to give up a job in New York that's very important to her."

"Maybe she *wants* to give it up. Maybe she really

wants to stay here with us. You made a mistake, Dad.''

''What I made is a mess,'' Cade admitted.

''You always tell us to clean up our messes,'' his oldest son reminded.

Out of the mouths of babes... There was only one way Cade could clean up this mess, and it would require Charlie's cooperation.

The strategy meeting droned on and on, and so did the senior partner. Randi checked her watch for the umpteenth time. Since when had making chocolate-chip cookies with Sean, Tim and Gregory become more rewarding than law?

Since she'd met Cade, kissed him, and fallen in love with him and his sons.

She'd received her first letter from Gregory and drawings from Tim and Sean yesterday. She'd cried much of the evening, mostly because there had been no note from Cade. What was she expecting? A miracle?

Miracles were few and far between.

She stared at the notes in front of her. She had to keep her mind on her work. That was why she'd come back to New York.

Not really, the voice of truth inside her scolded. *You came back because Cade doesn't love you.*

Abruptly the door to the conference room opened. Randi looked up, wondering if one of the other partners had decided to sit in. To her amazement, Cade walked in.

He was wearing a navy suit and carried a bouquet of red roses. "The receptionist left and told me to wait. I've been waiting since five and it's now seven. I really need to talk to the lady. Maybe you could take a break?"

The senior partner peered over his wire-rimmed glasses at Randi. "You know this man, Miranda?"

"Uh, yes. At least, I think so. He was dressed differently the last time I saw him."

The older man stood and gathered his papers. "I'll be in my office when you're finished." He stepped into the hall and closed the door.

Randi wasn't sure what to say or do. She still hurt from the way Cade had treated her before she left, and she didn't know why he was here. "Mr. Hancock must have been getting hungry or he would have thrown you out. He doesn't like to have his meetings interrupted."

"It would have taken five of him to throw me out. And I wasn't about to waste the rest of the night when I've wasted enough time already."

She stood, feeling at a disadvantage, feeling as if she were in a dream. Cade coming to New York, bringing roses... "I told the boys they could visit. I didn't expect a visit from you."

"That's not all you told them," Cade said, stepping closer, holding her still with the intensity in his eyes.

"I tried to be honest with them. I tried—"

He was close enough to touch her, but he didn't. "You told them you were leaving so we'd stop hurting, didn't you?"

"Yes," she murmured, feeling her legs tremble, feeling hope begin to bloom again.

"You were wrong. When you left, I hurt more than I've ever hurt. I want you to come back."

She'd hoped for more. She'd hoped— "Cade, it won't work. You know it won't."

"Why? Because you'll miss all this?" He gestured around the beautifully appointed office.

It was too late to hide anything from him. "No. Because I want to be more than a housekeeper and you don't want that."

"Maybe you're wrong. Maybe I've changed my mind. Maybe I've finally realized the right woman by my side could make a monumental difference in my life and my sons'."

The flare of desire in Cade's eyes had been there since the day they'd met. But she thought she saw more now. She prayed she did. "The right woman?"

"You, Miranda Sinclair. Only you. After you left, I realized if I didn't let go of the past, I wouldn't have a future—at least, not one filled with the happiness the boys and I deserve. Will you marry me, be my wife and mother to my sons?"

She almost said yes. But then she realized she needed to know exactly what Cade felt...because one-sided love would never be enough. "Why?"

He laid the flowers on the table and finally touched her, taking her hands in his. "Because I love you, Randi. You were right. I was afraid to love again. Even when it started happening, I denied it. But I've never felt for anyone what I feel for you. When you left..." He shook his head and brought her hand to his lips. The nerve worked in his jaw as he fought to control his emotion.

She traced his upper lip with her thumb. "Leaving you and the boys was the hardest thing I've ever done. But if you couldn't ask me to stay, I knew I had to leave."

He cleared his throat. "So now I'm asking you to stay with me, to love me, to make a life no matter how hard the snow falls, or the rains come, or..."

"For better or worse...for a lifetime. Yes, I'll marry you, Cade Gallagher."

Joy broke over his face as he lifted her into his arms and kissed her—at first with a gentle tenderness, then with an urgent desire that left them both breathless.

Slowly, he let her slide down his body. His need for her was as obvious as the sincerity in his face when he said, "I'm sorry, Randi. For that last night, and acting like a jealous lover...."

She touched her fingers to his lips. "You were fighting to protect yourself."

He cupped her chin in his hand. "I don't want to protect myself any longer."

Tucking her hands under his suitcoat and around his waist, she said, "I know you don't want to be away from the ranch for long. When are you flying back?"

"That depends. Can you resign immediately?" he asked slyly.

She smiled. "I should at least give Hancock a day's notice."

"I'll be generous. Give him two." Cade flashed a quick grin. "Will that really be enough?"

With no hesitation, she answered, "Yes. Since I came back, my heart really hasn't been in the work here. Hancock appointed another partner as head counsel on the case. I was simply giving my input. If they still need it, I can do it from the ranch. If not... What would you think about my setting up a practice in Hampton, once Sean starts school?"

"I want you to do what will make you happy."

"What will make us *both* happy. We're in this together, Cade."

He wrapped her in his arms again. "Yes, we are. Just keep reminding me so I don't forget."

Raising her lips to his, she reminded him with a kiss that spoke of commitment and promises and a lifetime of love.

Epilogue

On January first, Randi slowly started down the stairs, her white satin gown beaded with seed pearls flowing around her ankles. She and Cade had decided that no other day could be more fitting for their wedding, for a new beginning and a new life. Cade had pushed the living-room furniture to the perimeter of the room and set up folding chairs to accommodate family and friends. The evening before, New Year's Eve, Katie had helped Randi and the boys decorate while Cade, Jeff, Nathan and Gavin had spent a few hours in the bunkhouse reliving old times.

Now, as Randi descended the remaining few steps, she smiled at her father who'd finally agreed to come, Cade's parents, her brothers, Laura and

Ned, Al and Buck and Charlie, Katie, Jeff and Nathan. Sean, Tim and Gregory in their white shirts and ties beamed at her from the first row of chairs.

Gavin, Cade's best man, grinned and gave her a thumbs-up sign. Randi handed her bouquet of flowers to Katie. Then her gaze found Cade's. The love in his eyes wrapped around her, excited her, led her to step toward him with a smile on her face and tears in her eyes. He reached out to her, and she took his hand and stood beside him.

"You look beautiful," he murmured, squeezing her fingers.

Cade was dressed in a Western-cut tuxedo. He'd never looked more handsome, or strong, or proud. Since his trip to New York, he'd insisted they still sleep in separate bedrooms. He'd wanted their wedding night to be special. She admired him and loved him even more because he had done everything he could to make this day one to cherish.

Leaning close, he whispered in her ear. "I don't think two days and nights in a honeymoon suite in Billings will be nearly enough."

Excitement rippled through her, along with the sheer joy of loving Cade. She murmured very low, "We'll have every night in our bed for the rest of our lives."

From beside Cade, Gavin said, "Reverend, if you don't soon marry these two, they'll do it themselves."

Their friends laughed.

And the minister began.

Cade slipped his arm under Randi's veil and around her waist to hold her close.

When the minister came to the exchange of vows, he nodded to Cade.

Cade faced Randi, taking both her hands. His voice was steady and sure. "I promise to love you, cherish you, and protect you through the brightest days and the darkest nights. I will stand by you, care for you, and always try to solve our problems rather than run from them. I promise to try to see your point of view even when I don't agree. I will always be faithful, and every day I vow to give our love the respect it deserves."

Cade's vows were so like him—honest, basic, laced with a strength of character she knew would last their whole lives. She curved her fingers into his palm and held on to him. It was her turn.

"From this day on, I promise to love, honor, and respect you. I want to be your partner, your help-mate, and a mother to Sean, Tim, and Gregory as well as any other children we bring into the world."

Emotion blazed even stronger in Cade's eyes and the nerve in his jaw worked as she went on. "I promise to share my joys with you and my sorrows. I will try to tell you when something bothers me so you don't have to guess, and I will try to never fall asleep angry. I will love you through winter storms and summer rodeos. When you need comfort, I'll offer it, and when you need understanding, I will always try to understand. Cade, I give you my heart today because I know you'll cherish it as I will yours. I vow to love you as long as I live and after, if it's possible.''

''Randi.'' The reverence in Cade's voice brought tears to her eyes all over again.

Then they exchanged rings—his pledge deep and husky, hers low and shaky. After a blessing, the minister pronounced them husband and wife.

When Cade kissed her, their hearts bonded even more closely than their lives.

Applause rang out.

Cade lifted his head and then broke into a grin. ''Happy New Year, Mrs. Gallagher.''

Sean, Tim and Gregory gathered around them. Sean tugged on Randi's arm. ''Are we married now?''

She laughed and hugged all three boys. ''We're married. And we're a family.''

''Forever,'' Gregory pronounced.

Tim nodded. ''Forever.''

Randi gazed up at Cade. He held out his hand again, ready to start their lives together by greeting their guests. She took it, standing beside him, knowing that was where she would always be.

*   *   *   *   *

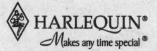

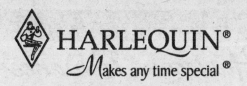

HARLEQUIN®
Makes any time special ®

AMERICAN *Romance*

Upbeat, All-American Romances

HARLEQUIN®
Duets™

Romantic Comedy

**Harlequin®
Historical**

Historical, Romantic Adventure

HARLEQUIN®
INTRIGUE

Romantic Suspense

Harlequin Romance®

Capturing the World You Dream Of

HARLEQUIN® *Presents*

Seduction and passion guaranteed

HARLEQUIN® *Super*ROMANCE®

Emotional, Exciting, Unexpected

HARLEQUIN®
Temptation®

Sassy, Sexy, Seductive!